'I don't understand why you career women always have to put down women who choose to stay home and take care of their families. You act as though it's some kind of imprisonme it or a punishment inflicted on them by chauvinistic men. Has it ever occurred to you that raising the next generation just might be as important as practising law or medicine? Weren't you implying that all women should have careers?' he shot back.

'Not really. I just don't see that family and career are necessarily incompatible.'

'Well, I think they are,' he said stiffly.

Books you will enjoy
by ROSEMARY HAMMOND

TWO DIFFERENT WORLDS

Nicole was a city girl who couldn't boil an egg; Dirk Morgan was the self-sufficient wilderness expert who rescued her from a snowstorm. While they were marooned in Dirk's cabin, the attraction between them grew, but it was an attraction of opposites—so how could it last once they were back in their two different worlds?

BITTERSWEET REVENGE

When Michael Prescott blamed Val for his brother's death, she was distressed and outraged. But that reaction paled into insignificance when she was faced with Michael's deliberate plan of revenge. What a fool she had been to finally trust a man!

THE WRONG KIND OF MAN

Nora always fell for the wrong kind of man— slim, blond city-slicker types—and she always got hurt. So when she met Mark Leighton, who was dark and strong and a farmer and *very* straightforward, her problems ought to have been solved. Mark certainly liked Nora. But she just couldn't seem to feel *that way* about him...

ANYTHING FOR YOU

BY

ROSEMARY HAMMOND

MILLS & BOON LIMITED
ETON HOUSE 18-24 PARADISE ROAD
RICHMOND SURREY TW9 1SR

First published in Great Britain 1991
by Mills & Boon Limited

© Rosemary Hammond 1991

Australian copyright 1991
Philippine copyright 1991
This edition 1991

ISBN 0 263 77060 5

Set in Times Roman 10½ on 12 pt.
01-9104-50971 C

Made and printed in Great Britain

CHAPTER ONE

REGAN sat in the plush waiting-room of the city's largest and most prestigious law firm, trying to conceal her nervous jitters. It was her third interview of the day, and, while the other two had virtually made her firm offers, it was the Courtney & Wainwright firm she had her heart set on.

Her spine was rigid against the straight back of the chair, her legs pressed together, sensibly shod feet planted squarely on the thick carpet, the skirt of her tailored tweed suit decorously covering her knees. Rule number one for women trying to break into a male profession: never appear frivolous or provocative.

She shifted the strap of her leather handbag on her shoulder. Maybe it had been a mistake to bring one. How in the world did men carry everything they needed in their pockets? She didn't know what to do with it: set it on the floor by her feet, hold it in her lap, or keep it where it was. In it was the letter she had received yesterday confirming her interview.

'Dear Mr McIntyre,' the salutation had read. Once again, she was *Mr* McIntyre. She should have become accustomed to the error by now, but it still made her feel uneasy, even a little guilty. She had searched in vain for a way to spell it out on her résumé that she was a woman, but, short of typing in the blunt statement 'I AM FEMALE' at some auspicious point, never came up with a clever way to do it.

It wasn't her fault her father had thought he was King Lear. At least she'd had two sisters before her to get stuck with Cordelia and Goneril. Poor Goneril! She'd suffered with her name, too.

She glanced sideways at the two young men sitting at either end of the long leather couch opposite her. From their youthful appearance, they were obviously applicants, too. *They* didn't have handbags to worry about or knees to cover.

One of them was lolling back, one leg crossed over the other, gazing out the window behind Regan at the spectacular view of Puget Sound, the busy harbour twenty storeys below, the snowy mountains in the background. The other was leaning forward, legs spread apart, leafing casually through the *Wall Street Journal*.

Just as Regan was about to move her bag from her shoulder to her lap, simply to have something to do with her hands, a tall, efficient-looking blonde came out into the waiting-room and glanced at the three of them sitting there.

Regan's stomach turned over, and she clenched the muscles tight to hold back the incipient gurgle she sensed was about to erupt. It was two o'clock in the afternoon, and she hadn't eaten since breakfast, a mere half-slice of toast. She'd been too nervous for anything more substantial.

'Regan McIntyre?' the blonde called out in a bored, haughty tone, her eyes fastening on the two men.

Regan jumped to her feet. 'Yes,' she said in a voice she knew was too loud. 'That's me.'

The blonde raised her perfectly arched eyebrows, and once again Regan cursed the ambiguous name her Shakespeare-loving father had given her. It seemed she'd been explaining all her life, twenty-seven long years, that she was a girl, not a boy.

'I'm Nick Wainwright's secretary,' the blonde said in a tone that made Regan feel she should bow down or salute. 'Follow me.'

Regan hurried after her down a wide corridor past a library where about ten men and one lone woman were seated at tables stacked high with thick volumes and scribbling on lined yellow legal pads, then on to a corner office. The door was open, and the secretary walked inside. After a moment's hesitation, Regan followed.

A man was sitting at a large desk, facing away from them and looking out of the window. He was leaning back in a dark green swivel chair, his feet propped up on the credenza against the wall, and talking on the telephone in a clipped, curt voice. All Regan could see of him was that he had very dark hair and broad shoulders under a well-tailored dark suit.

The blonde stepped over to the desk, and the moment there was a lull in the conversation, she said in a loud voice, 'Regan McIntyre is here to see you.'

Without turning around, the dark-haired man only waved a hand in the air to acknowledge the announcement. The secretary, her job apparently done, turned on her heel and walked past Regan back out into the hall, closing the door quietly behind her.

Regan stood there waiting, eyeing the two smaller chairs on her side of the desk and wondering if she dared to sit down without an invitation. While she debated, she glanced around the room. It was unlike any of the offices she'd seen so far on her rounds of interviews.

It looked more like a room in a home than an office, with heavy antique mahogany furniture, highly polished and beautifully cared for. There was an enormous break-front against one wall, with bright brass fittings, glass doors on the top and leather volumes on the shelves behind them. On the walls were the usual framed diplomas, but there were also three or four really fine drawings, and one lovely water-colour, an abstract design that appeared vaguely floral in concept.

Just then the door opened, and a grey-haired, rather portly man walked inside. He was carrying a manila file folder. When he saw Regan, he stopped short, and his face registered the same surprise as the secretary's had. He glanced quickly at the folder, then smiled at her and held out a hand.

'Regan McIntyre, I presume,' he said as they shook hands. 'I'm James Courtney, the firm's managing partner.'

Regan smiled at the predictable response. 'How do you do?' she said.

'Won't you sit down?' He glanced at the dark-haired man, still deep in his conversation. 'That's Nick Wainwright, my partner. He seems to spend most of his life on the telephone. I keep telling him he should look into the possibility of having a receiver transplanted into his ear.'

Regan laughed. James Courtney, as managing partner, was the one who would make the decision whether to employ her. He had put her so much at ease with his kindly offhand manner that she even began to hope that maybe...

'Now,' Mr Courtney said, when they were seated. 'Your credentials are impressive, *Miss* McIntyre.' He gave her an enquiring look. 'Or do you prefer Ms?'

Regan shook her head. 'Miss is fine. I'm not fussy.'

He nodded and flipped through the file on his lap. 'Let's see, Stanford graduate, highest marks, chosen for *Law Review*, some of the best recommendations I've seen.' He looked at her. 'I notice that you specialised in antitrust courses in law school, and Judge Fremont speaks very highly of the work you did for him your last year. That was invaluable experience, clerking for a federal judge.'

'Yes. Judge Fremont handles most of the antitrust cases in the Ninth Circuit.'

'It sounds as though you're just what we're looking for. Of course, we do have others to interview, and my friend Wainwright over there will really have the final say, since he's our big antitrust gun, but I think he'll be as impressed with your background as I am. However, you do understand that, as in most large firms, you'll probably be transferred around eventually so that you can become familiar with other aspects of the law.'

At that moment, the telephone receiver was banged down, and, with a muttered curse under his breath, the man swivelled around to face them.

'That damned judge down in San Francisco has——' he began. Then he stopped short and stared at Regan. His eyes narrowed and shifted to James Courtney, one eyebrow raised in a mute question.

'Nick,' the older man said. 'This is Regan McIntyre. If you remember, we were both impressed with her résumé. I think she'll do for what you need.'

Regan smiled brightly at the dark-haired man, but when she saw his face darken in a look of open hostility her smile faded. His square jaw was clamped shut, the heavy eyebrows lowering over eyes that were mere slits, and he almost seemed poised to spring across the desk and attack her at any moment.

'*This* is Regan McIntyre?' he asked at last in an incredulous tone that was heavy with sarcasm. He shook his head firmly. 'No, Jim. It won't do. You know it won't do.' He rose abruptly to his feet, stood behind the desk towering over them and shot Regan another black look. 'No offence, *Miss* McIntyre, but I can't work with a woman.'

He sat back down, just as abruptly, picked up the telephone and began to dial. Apparently, the subject was closed, through all eternity.

Regan glanced at James Courtney. His face was flushed with barely suppressed anger, and he was obviously struggling for control. Finally, he sighed, rose slowly to his feet and smiled down at her.

'Come on, Miss McIntyre. I'll sort this out myself later. I want you to know that it is not our firm's policy to discriminate against any applicant, not on the basis of race or religion, and definitely not on the basis of sex. It's time our Mr Wainwright learned that.'

Out in the hall, Regan didn't know quite what to do or say or even how to take Nick Wainwright's blunt rejection. She was angry, humiliated, and cowed by him all at the same time. She wanted to go back inside the office and challenge him, but she also wanted to run away and hide.

'I apologise for Nick's bad manners,' James Courtney was saying. He took her by the elbow and started walking her down the corridor towards the reception room. 'He has a blind spot about women attorneys.'

Regan's heart plummeted. All she felt now was a terrible disappointment. She had coveted that job, the firm of her choice, but most of all she had wanted to work with Nick Wainwright, whose reputation in antitrust circles was legendary. She could learn so much from him. How was she to have known he'd turn out to be a male chauvinist pig, one of those arrogant bigots who couldn't see beyond his own prejudices?

'I'm sorry, too, Mr Courtney,' she said stiffly. 'I thought the days of bias against women in the law were over long ago.'

'And so they are,' he replied. 'Except in some quarters,' he added grimly under his breath.

They were back in the reception-room. The two young men were still sitting there, and they looked up expectantly as Regan and James Courtney walked past them towards the bank of lifts.

Regan punched the down button and turned to the older man. 'Well, thanks anyway,' she said, holding out her hand. 'You've been very kind.'

He eyed her carefully. 'I don't want to get your hopes up,' he said in a low voice, 'but I do want you to know that I'm on your side, and I'm going to do everything within my power to drill some sense into Wainwright's thick head.'

The lift arrived just then, and Regan stepped inside. Just before the doors slid closed, James Courtney nodded and gave her a warm smile.

'In any event,' he said, 'you'll be hearing from us shortly, one way or the other.'

*   *   *

'Well, Dad, I hope you're happy,' Regan said into the telephone. 'That whimsical name you gave me just lost me a job today.'

She was stretched out on the couch in the living-room of her small apartment on Capitol Hill, the telephone sitting on her chest, the receiver stuck between her cheek and her shoulder, filing her nails.

'I don't know what you're talking about,' her father said stiffly. 'I gave all three of you girls lovely names.'

'I hardly think poor Goneril would agree with you. It sounds more like a disease than a woman's name.'

'If you're referring to your sister Gerry, I haven't heard her complaining. And Delia seems quite happy with her name.'

'That's because they can at least shorten them. No one has called them Goneril or Cordelia since before they were born. Lucky for them Mother had the good sense to change them into something human. But what can you do with Regan?'

'It's a perfectly nice name,' he said in a lofty tone.

'Sure, for a man.'

'"How sharper than a serpent's tooth it is,"' he quoted distantly, '"to have a thankless child."'

'Oh, Dad,' she groaned. 'Not Shakespeare again. You are *not* King Lear, Father, dear.'

'I know that,' was the dignified reply.

She giggled into the telephone. 'Sometimes I wonder.'

'Seriously, did you really lose the job because of your name, honey?'

'No, of course not. In fact it went quite well up to a point. I thought I had it in the bag until the man I'd be working for took one look at me and realised

I wasn't a man.' She sighed. 'He's one of *those*, if you know what I mean.'

'How about the other interviews? Any hot prospects?'

'As a matter of fact, yes. They both called when I got home late this afternoon and made offers.'

'Will you accept one of them?'

'Oh, I suppose so. I need to start earning some money, and the pay is fantastic. It's just that . . .'

'Oh, come on, honey. Cheer up. You're a bright girl. One of these days the man who turned you down will come crawling on his hands and knees begging you to go to work for him.'

'Oh, Dad,' she said with a laugh. 'You do know how to bolster my morale.'

'That's what a father's for,' he said smugly.

'Even if he does think he's King Lear,' she added slyly.

'I do *not* think——' he spluttered.

The doorbell buzzed just then, cutting him off.

'I have to go now, Dad. Someone's at the door. I'll call you next week after I've made up my mind which job to take.'

When she'd hung up the telephone, she padded barefoot to the door, which was firmly locked and fastened with a chain bolt.

'Yes,' she called. 'Who is it?'

'It's Nick Wainwright,' came the prompt reply.

For a moment she couldn't place him. When it dawned on her just who was standing on the other side of the door, her mouth fell open. Stunned into immobility, she gazed down at her faded jeans, rumpled sweatshirt and bare feet in horror. Then she turned for a quick glance around the tiny living-room, which was a total disaster. She'd been so busy lately, polishing her résumé, making the rounds of law firms, studying for the Bar exam, that she'd scarcely had time to eat, much less clean.

There was nothing she could do now about the textbooks piled on the floor, the desk, the couch, in fact every available surface. Or the gaping grey box from the takeaway, the half-eaten pizza inside, its fragrant aroma still filling the room.

'Miss McIntyre,' came the impatient voice. 'Are you there?'

There was no way she could get dressed in something decent, comb her shoulder-length brown hair, put on some discreet make-up and clean up the room in one hour, much less the one minute she dared make him wait. But she wouldn't have to let him in.

She smoothed down the baggy shirt, ran her fingers through her hair, and slipped on the pair of moccasins she had discarded just inside the door when she came home with the pizza. Taking a deep breath, she opened the door and stepped out into the dimly lit hallway.

The first thing she noticed was how tall he was standing up. She was no half-pint herself, clocking in at five-feet-eight the last time she had measured, but he had to be six or seven inches taller, especially when she wasn't wearing heels.

She looked up at him. 'Yes, Mr Wainwright?'

'I'd like to talk to you,' he said curtly.

'All right.'

He paused and glanced around. 'Out here in the hall?'

'I—uh—I wasn't expecting anyone, and . . .' she stammered.

He raised an eyebrow. 'I see,' he said grimly. 'You have company. We can talk another time.'

He turned to go. Clearly he thought she was entertaining a man inside her apartment. Without thinking, she reached out and grabbed him by the arm. He whirled around and glared at her, and she dropped her hand as though it had been burned.

'No,' she said. 'It's not like that. It's just that I haven't had a chance to do much cleaning lately, and...'

'Listen,' he said impatiently, 'I'm not here to judge your housekeeping. As a matter of fact, I'm only here to discuss the job with our firm. I don't have to come in at all.'

'What about the job?' she asked warily.

'You've got it, if you still want it.'

She gaped up at him blankly. Was he serious? Did he really want her? Who cared? Fighting down the impulse to jump up and down and clap her hands like a schoolgirl, she controlled her elation and tried to look dignified and businesslike.

'I see.' She longed to quiz him about the reason for his sudden change of heart, but somehow had the feeling that the offer could very well be withdrawn if she asked one question.

It took him less than a minute to fill her in on the starting salary and other benefits, but she only listened with half an ear. She didn't care about any of those things. All she wanted was the chance to work with Nick Wainwright.

'Well?' he said when he was finished. 'Do you want the job or don't you?'

'Yes, I do,' she said without a second's hesitation. 'When do I start?'

'Today is Friday. Come in first thing Monday morning.'

'I'll be there.'

He nodded briefly at her, then turned around and strode off down the hall. Still stunned, she stared after him until he disappeared from view down the staircase. Thankfully, he didn't turn around once to catch her gaping after him.

Back inside the apartment, she closed the door, locked it, shot the chain bolt, then leaned back and closed her eyes. She hadn't a clue what had happened to change his mind. It was the last thing she had expected. This afternoon the subject had seemed to be definitely closed as far as he was concerned.

It had to have been James Courtney. Something he had said. Whatever it had been, the argument must have really worried him for him to have come to her apartment personally! Possibly the threat of a discrimination suit. She felt a little guilty about that, since it would never occur to her to do such a thing.

Still, she wasn't going to argue with success. However she had got the job, under whatever terms, it was what she wanted. Monday! she thought. She'd start work on Monday! She ran to the telephone to call her father.

Promptly at nine o'clock on Monday morning, Regan presented herself at the reception desk of the Courtney & Wainwright law offices. Behind the desk sat a plump-faced young woman with curly red hair. A pair of earphones was clamped on her head, and she was extremely busy plugging and unplugging telephone connections into a switchboard.

While she waited for a lull in the activity, Regan glanced out the wide bank of windows to the left. It was a lovely spring day in early May, the sun shining, the flowering cherries in blossom, a harbinger, Regan was certain, of her good fortune.

She had dressed with special care that morning in a dark blue tailored suit, white silk blouse and blue and red paisley scarf tied at the collar, the professional woman's uniform. Medium-heeled navy shoes and her leather handbag completed the outfit.

Her light brown hair was tucked decorously behind her ears, and she wore only a trace of subdued make-up. Her only jewellery was a wristwatch with a narrow black band. The last thing she wanted was to give Nick Wainwright any excuse to accuse her of provocative or 'feminine' behaviour. As far as he was concerned, she couldn't afford to be a woman at all. She'd have to act and dress and think as much like a man as possible.

The receptionist finally looked up from her switchboard. 'May I help you?' she asked.

'Yes, I'm Regan McIntyre. I'm to start work here today for Mr Wainwright.'

The girl smiled. 'Oh, hi. I'm Betsy. Just a second. I'll tell Sheila you're here.'

In a few moments the tall blonde secretary came out to the desk. Her expression was quite pleasant, and she didn't seem nearly so haughty or intimidating to Regan this morning as she had on Friday. Although she was beautifully put together, with an intricate professional hairstyle and wearing an expensively simple woollen dress, the clever make-up job didn't quite conceal the age lines on her face. Regan guessed she must be forty or more.

'Good morning,' the blonde said. 'I'm Sheila, Nick Wainwright's secretary.'

'And I'm Regan.'

Sheila's mouth twitched. 'You had us all fooled with that name.'

Regan made a face. 'The bane of my existence.'

'Oh, it's a nice name. Just a bit confusing. Come with me and I'll show you to your office.'

Regan followed her down the same wide corridor, past the library, which was busy even at this early hour. As they passed by, Regan was uncomfortably aware of several curious glances darted her way. It was only natural, she supposed, to inspect anyone new.

Finally they came to Nick Wainwright's corner office. The door was closed. Sheila glanced back at Regan over her shoulder.

'He has clients with him this morning,' she said in a muted voice. 'He asked me to help you get settled.'

She continued on to the room next door. Inside, Regan glanced around in dismay. It seemed more like a cupboard than an office, but that could have been because virtually every available wall surface was covered with heavy brown metal filing cabinets. There was no window. Against the far wall was a battered wooden desk, piled high with heavy red file folders.

'It's not much,' Sheila remarked ruefully, 'but it's the best I could come up with at such short notice, and Nick wanted you close by. He asked me to get out those files for you to go through.' She hesitated for a moment, then said, 'I suppose it's no secret to you that he's not exactly sensitive to the idea of women in the law profession.' She laughed shortly. 'In *any* profession, I might add.'

'I gathered that in the interview on Friday,' Regan replied drily. 'If you can call it that.'

'Well, don't let him get under your skin.'

Regan smiled. 'I'll try.' Then, curious, she asked, 'How long have you worked for him, Sheila?'

'Let's see, it'll be seven years in August.'

'You must know him quite well by now, then. Maybe you can tell me why he hates women so much.'

Sheila's eyes widened in shock. 'Nick? Hate women? Believe me, nothing could be further from the truth. He treats everyone like that, male or female, at least on the job. It's just his way. He's very demanding when it comes to his work, but...' She laughed in genuine amusement. 'That's really funny, the idea that Nick dislikes women. Actually, if any man ever reaped the benefits from the women's liberation movement, it's Nick Wainwright.'

'What do you mean?'

Sheila shrugged. 'Well, you'll have to admit that the sexual revolution—you know, since the Pill—has taken a lot of the hard work out of seduction for men.'

Regan stared thoughtfully at her. She'd been far too busy in the last seven or eight years, working her way through four years of college and three years of law school, to bother much about her sex life. Good scholarships were hard to come by and the competition for them so fierce that she'd spent most of her spare time studying.

Sheila visibly stiffened under Regan's steady gaze. 'Listen, I'm sorry,' she said brusquely. 'I should know by now when to keep my big mouth shut. I'm afraid I'm still not quite used to thinking of women as lawyers, you know, part of the Establishment, and just naturally reacted to you as I would another secretary.'

Regan put a hand on her arm. 'Listen, Sheila,' she said in a sober voice, 'this is all new to me, too. All I want is to do a good job. I hope we can be friends. Certainly nothing you say to me in confidence will ever get back to Nick Wainwright.'

Sheila relaxed visibly. 'Well, that's all right, then. Nick and I have a fine working relationship, and I want to keep it that way.'

'What's he like to work for?' Regan asked.

'Well, except for a temper that flares up now and then and a tendency to make unreasonable demands, he's the best boss I've ever had,' Sheila replied with feeling. 'But then I'm a secretary, not another lawyer. Although, to give the devil his due, I doubt if he'll be any harder on you, just because you're a woman, than he is on any of the other young lawyers. He's just very demanding. He sets high standards for himself, and expects everyone else to meet them. Sometimes that doesn't work.'

'Am I the only woman attorney the firm has hired?' Regan asked slowly.

'Oh, no. There are at least four or five others besides you. But, since Nick ordinarily won't have anything to do with them, I haven't had that much contact with them.'

The telephone on the desk shrilled just then and Regan jumped. Sheila gave her a questioning look, then went over to the desk and picked up the receiver.

'Miss McIntyre's office,' she said in a smooth, businesslike tone. She listened for a moment, then said, 'Right away,' and hung up. She looked at Regan.

'The master's voice,' she commented drily. 'He wants me in his office. I'll leave you to settle in. He'll probably be around later to see how you're doing.'

When Sheila was gone, Regan took one last despairing look around the cramped little office, then sat down on the shabby chair behind the desk. It squeaked under her weight and a loose spring jabbed her sharply in the bottom, making her jump.

Her earlier feeling of joyful anticipation had pretty much dissipated by now, and a dull wave of depression threatened. She had no idea what to do with herself or what was expected of her. You'd think he'd have the decency to greet her on her first day, she grumbled to herself. At least give her a clue what he wanted her to do. Go over the files, Sheila had said.

She settled down and opened the first folder. Just then the telephone rang again. Gingerly she lifted it.

'Regan McIntyre,' she said in a small voice.

'Jim Courtney here,' came the pleasant voice. 'Just wanted to check to make sure you're getting settled all right.'

'Yes,' she said quickly. 'Sheila has been a big help.'

'Sorry about the terrible office. Nick insists on having all his files close at hand, and, since you'll be working with him, he thought it best to put you in there for the time being.'

'Oh, it's fine, really,' she said. 'No problem.'

'Well, if Nick doesn't need you right now, you'd better come down to the business office and check in with our personnel people. There are endless tax and insurance forms to fill out. Then I'll take you around to meet some of the others.'

* * *

Regan spent all that morning and most of the afternoon getting acclimatised and signing forms. Everyone
she met seemed friendly, but there were so many new
faces she didn't see how she'd begin to remember all
their names.

Back in her office later that afternoon, she started
going through the filing cabinets in an attempt to
acquaint herself with Nick's cases, but she had no
idea where to begin without some direction from him.
What did he want her to do? Surely, if she had been
hired to be his assistant, he must have some specific
task in mind for her. If so, he was keeping it a secret.

Finally, it was six o'clock, and she still hadn't seen
anything of Nick Wainwright throughout the entire
day except for a few glimpses of his retreating back
in the hallway. The office was quiet, virtually empty
after the mass exodus at five o'clock. Should she go
home? Or was she supposed to wait for his
permission?

She went out into the hall and peered around. His
door was still closed. Not a sound came from the
office behind it. Yet she knew he was still there. She
would have seen him if he'd left. She debated for
several seconds. Then, feeling like a schoolgirl at the
head's office, she squared her shoulders, raised her
hand, and rapped lightly on the door.

'Come in,' came the faint, curt command.

She opened the door and walked inside. He was
sitting behind his desk, bending over a thick stack of
papers, frowning heavily in concentration. Although
he was in his shirt-sleeves, he looked as well-groomed,
as immaculate, as he had the first time she'd seen him.
She stood in front of the desk waiting.

Finally he looked up. He stared at her blankly for a moment, as though trying to place her. Then the frown deepened into a dark scowl, and when he spoke, his tone was abrupt.

'Yes, what is it, McIntyre?'

'Er—I was wondering if you needed me any more today, Mr Wainwright.'

'What for?'

She spread her hands. 'Well, that's what I wanted to...'

He shook his head, and his mouth curled slightly at the edges. 'No,' he said in a mocking tone. 'I don't need you.'

Then he bent his head over his papers again, obviously dismissing her. Regan felt anger blazing up inside her like a hot flame. She clenched her fists at her sides and ground her back teeth together to keep from shouting at him or throwing something at him.

She turned on her heel and stalked out of the room, exerting a supreme effort not to slam the door behind her. Back in her own little cubbyhole next door, she stared blankly at the battered desk, the tottering filing cabinets, then stooped down to collect her handbag.

'So that's his game,' she muttered aloud. 'He was forced to hire me, but he'll try to freeze me out by ignoring me. We'll just have to see about that.'

All the way down the empty corridor, the lift ride to the lobby of the building, the walk to her bus stop, the trip home, during her shower, her meagre supper, and later lying in bed that night, Regan's one thought was to concoct a way to make Mr Nick Conceited Wainwright eat his words. As she plotted and planned, however, she always ended up with the same conclusion: the only possible course open to her was to somehow prove her worth to him.

It wasn't going to be easy. She'd have to get his attention first.

CHAPTER TWO

'GO OVER the files,' Regan muttered under her breath as she flopped herself down at her shabby desk next morning. All right, if that was what Nick Wainwright wanted, that was what she'd do. And in the end she'd find a way to make him acknowledge her existence.

Actually, it was an interesting case, although extremely complex, as antitrust matters tended to be. Nick represented a local pharmaceutical firm, one of several plaintiffs in a suit against three huge chemical laboratories, which, his client claimed, were involved in a conspiracy to fix prices.

The work was tedious, consisting mainly of sifting through the tons of documents produced by the three defendants, looking for proof of collusion among them, but it was a labour of love for Regan, the kind of detail work she was good at, and there was always the thrill of victory when such evidence was discovered.

She spent the next three days at the task, arriving at her desk before eight in the morning and not leaving until after seven at night. By Friday, she had made page after page of notes in her neat handwriting and was ready for the second phase of her campaign to get Nick Wainwright's attention.

During that entire week he hadn't spoken one word to her. She'd hardly seen him except for his rare appearances as he strode past her open door on his way somewhere else. Nor had she even heard his voice except occasionally through their common wall, and then usually raised in anger.

When she finished drafting the memo to him, she went in search of Sheila. Closeted in the tiny office all week, buried in the endless stacks of file folders, she had no idea what she was supposed to do for her typing. If Sheila wouldn't come to her rescue, she'd have to ask Jim Courtney for help, and she wanted to save him as a last resort, since he seemed to be the only person who had any influence over Nick.

Predictably, Sheila occupied the small office on the other side of Nick's. There was a connecting door between them, which was shut tight. The blonde secretary was seated at her desk, typing rapidly. Regan knocked lightly on the door and stepped inside.

'Sheila, I'm here to throw myself on your mercy.'

Sheila straightened up and flexed her fingers. 'What can I do for you?' she asked.

'Is there a stray typewriter around that I can use?' She held up her notes.

Sheila shook her head firmly. 'No,' she said in a severe tone. 'Don't start out that way.' She leaned forward and gave Regan a conspiratorial look. 'Let me clue you in. There's a definite pecking order around here. New lawyers aren't assigned secretaries until they've proved themselves, but they *never* do their own typing.'

Regan smiled. 'Sounds like catch twenty-two. What am I supposed to do? Write everything out in longhand?'

Sheila reached out a hand. 'What have you got?'

Regan gave her the legal pad. 'It's a memo to Mr Wainwright about the research I've been doing on the pharmaceutical case.'

Sheila flipped through the pages, then set it down on top of the desk. 'OK,' she said. 'If I don't have time for it, I'll find someone else to type it for you.'

Regan breathed a grateful sigh of relief. That was one hurdle crossed. 'Oh, bless you, Sheila,' she said with feeling. 'That would be great.'

'When do you need it?'

'Today would be nice, but there's no real hurry.' She nodded at the door. 'He doesn't seem to be waiting on tenterhooks for any input from me.'

Suddenly from behind the closed door came a loud roar. 'Sheila!'

Sheila rolled her eyes, grabbed a shorthand pad and pencil off her desk and rose to her feet. 'Speak of the devil,' she said drily. 'See you later.'

From that day on, Regan bombarded him with memos, sometimes two a day. Since he never responded to them or acknowledged them in any way, she had no idea whether her analyses and comments on the case were helpful or a load of utter drivel, but she continued to crank them out anyway. It was her only hope.

Sheila was usually too busy to help her, but in time came up with a mousy little girl named Suzy, who apparently served as a floater, helping the lawyers who had no regular secretaries. Suzy was slow and not much of a speller, but she was willing and almost always available.

By the end of two weeks, Regan was just about ready to give it up as hopeless. Her painstaking work still hadn't elicited the slightest response from the man next door. She had, however, learned a great deal about him from her co-workers. He was a near-legendary figure, not only for his legal expertise, but, if office gossip were true, for his reputation with women.

So far there had been only vague hints about this proclivity of his, but it wasn't until that very morning that it was actually brought out into the open. A group of the younger lawyers were gathered in the coffee-room for their customary short break, when someone, one of the men, Regan recalled later, started it.

'By the way, what's the latest on Old Nick's love-life?' he asked casually out of the blue.

Immediately a hush descended on the table. Regan sensed that the others were darting expectant looks at her. She almost choked on her coffee. Surely they didn't think that she...?

'What do you mean?' she asked when she'd finished coughing. 'I don't know what you're talking about.'

Margaret Pierce, a rather serious, attractive redhead, only a few years older than Regan, leaned across the table, her hazel eyes glinting.

'You're his assistant,' she said, her low tone of voice loaded with meaning. 'Surely you can tell us who the current flame is?'

Regan laughed drily. 'You must be joking. The man hasn't spoken two words to me since I came to work here.' By now her curiosity was aroused. 'It sounds as though he's pretty—um—active in that direction.'

They all started talking at once. Each had a story to tell, or his or her own unique version of the same story, and all Regan could really make out of the gabble was that Old Nick, as they continued to call him, was considered one of the city's most eligible bachelors who had never even come close to marriage.

Yet she also gathered that he kept his love-life and his professional life strictly separate. Hence the reason they tackled her for information.

As she listened to their revelations, she had to wonder how much of it was true. Even though Sheila had hinted at his reputation, she couldn't quite picture him in the role of Lothario. She couldn't even have given an accurate description of him, except that he was tall, had dark hair and a nasty disposition.

A young man named Dan was speaking now. 'I've even tried to corner Sheila on the subject, but if she knows anything she's not breathing a word.'

'That's loyalty for you,' Margaret said.

Regan was just about to ask them why in the world they even cared about the man's personal life, when all of a sudden a familiar barking voice rang out behind her, cutting into the chatter.

'McIntyre!'

There was an immediate silence in the room. Startled, Regan jerked her head around, spilling the dregs of her coffee on the table in the process. Frantically mopping at the mess with paper napkins, she stumbled to her feet and turned to face him.

'Yes, sir,' she mumbled.

'In my office,' he said, then turned and walked out of the room.

Regan finished cleaning off the table, gave the others a look of mock despair, which wasn't entirely an act, and hurried after him down the hallway.

He was already sitting down behind his desk, poring over some papers, when she got to his office. Without looking up, he raised a hand and pointed in the distance behind her.

'Close the door.'

She did so.

'Sit down.'

She perched gingerly on the edge of one of the chairs and waited for the axe to fall. The memory of the comments made in the coffee-room was still fresh in her mind, and while she waited, watching him, she examined him closely.

Old Nick? She almost broke into nervous giggles at that. He wasn't old at all. Possibly thirty-five or -six. She'd look it up later in the Attorneys' Directory. But a womaniser? Did he look the part? He certainly wasn't handsome. His jaw was too square, the planes of his face too flat, the mouth too thin for that.

He had a nice head of dark hair, smooth and thick, a shade too long, and he dressed well, always in dark conservative suits and white shirts. She didn't know the colour of his eyes, since every time he looked at her they were narrowed in a scowl.

He did have a charming nose, she decided, straight, classic, not too large, certainly not small. In fact, she finally came to the grudging conclusion that, taking him all in all, he might be considered quite attractive— if he ever smiled. She'd certainly seen no evidence of good humour in him.

At that moment he raised his head and their eyes met. Grey, she thought. His eyes were a deep slate colour. Before she could look away he had raised one dark eyebrow inquiringly.

'Something wrong, McIntyre?' he asked with deceptive gentleness.

She shook her head vigorously. 'No, sir. No. Not at all. I was just...' Her voice trailed away. 'Just thinking,' she added weakly.

He leaned back in his chair and picked up the papers he had been studying. It was then that Regan realised they were the memos she had been sending him, and she reddened. It was quite a handful. She hadn't realised there were quite so many.

'These notes of yours,' he said, waving them in the air.

'Yes?'

'They're damned good.'

If he had suddenly lunged across the desk and knocked her off her chair she couldn't have been more stunned. Good? Could he be serious? Her head was spinning so crazily she didn't even realise he was still speaking to her, but when his voice finally penetrated, she concentrated hard on every word.

'You've obviously made a thorough study of the case,' he went on in the same flat, grudging tone. 'Now, I've never made any secret of the fact that I don't like working with women. They're emotional, unpredictable, and generally undependable, and I've seen several such collaborations lead to disaster. Nothing,' he said, 'nothing at all must interfere with the conduct of a case.'

He banged his fist on the desk for emphasis, and Regan jumped half out of her chair.

'Oh, I quite agrée,' she hastened to assure him.

'All right then, since it looks as though you can do the job, and we are after all paying your salary, you might as well earn it. Now, here's what I want you to do.'

He shoved a legal pad and a pencil across the desk at her, obviously expecting her to take notes, and for the next two hours he went over the case with her, spelling out his strategy, filling her in on what he expected from her, pausing only briefly every now and then to give her time to ask a question.

By the end of the session Regan's fingers were cramped and her head seemed to be full of cotton wool, but, when he dismissed her with a curt nod, she went next door to her little office filled with a sense of wild elation. He trusted her! He was going to let her work with him!

During the next three weeks, Regan's enthusiasm gradually began to dissipate as it slowly dawned on her that, far from working *with* Nick Wainwright in any collaborative effort, she was rapidly becoming nothing more than his slave.

At least he talked to her now. In fact, the very next morning when she had arrived at her office there he had been, standing by her desk and shuffling through several neat stacks of files that hadn't been there the night before. As she had walked slowly towards him, he had glanced meaningfully at his watch.

'I've been waiting for you,' he said in an accusing tone.

She stared at him. 'It's only eight o'clock.'

'If you want to be a successful lawyer, you have to be prepared to make little sacrifices.' Before she could say a word, he continued, 'These documents arrived late last night. They're from one of our opponents in the pharmaceutical case. They need to be stamped and photocopied. Two copies each. Then read through them and make a list of pertinent information.'

Regan set her handbag on the floor beside her chair and looked down at the tall piles of documents in utter bewilderment.

'What am I looking for?' she asked finally.

'Anything we can use,' was the brusque reply.

With that, he turned and stalked out. Regan gazed after him. Naturally, she was pleased that he had sought out her help at last, but would it really hurt him to be just a little more specific about what it was he wanted? What did he expect? Did he think she was a mind reader?

There was an intricate metal stamping machine and an ink pad sitting on her desk. She picked up the machine, which was set to number ahead consecutively, and examined it with distaste. Stamp the documents. Run off two copies. Make a list. Tote that barge. Lift that bale. Was this why she had spent three years in law school?

She sat down and started stamping.

Day by day it became clearer to Regan that all she was accomplishing was the flunkey work Sheila was too busy to do, and, by the end of three weeks, her hands were cramped from pounding the stamping machine, her feet were sore from standing at the copier for hours on end, and she was ready to throw in the towel. Either that or murder Nick Wainwright.

She did, however, finally finish, even to making up the list of pertinent information contained in the documents he'd requested. It had been typed neatly by Suzy, after four revisions, and that afternoon Regan took it into Nick's office when she knew he'd be gone and threw it on his desk.

Then she went back to her own room and sat down to compose her letter of resignation. She'd had all she could take. If he merely wanted a dogsbody to do his dirty work, he could hire one at a much cheaper rate than he paid her. Her salary was a waste of the firm's money, and she intended to include that observation in her letter.

When it was drafted, she felt much better, but, after reading it over, she decided it might be wise to let it simmer for a while. It was a drastic move, and she really should think it over, perhaps even discuss it with Jim Courtney or one of the other young lawyers before actually submitting it.

Before she could change her mind, she shoved it into the top drawer of her desk and started off down the hall to the coffee-room. After three weeks of unremitting hard work, she deserved a break.

The only occupants of the room were two of the other women lawyers in the firm, sitting together silently at one of the round tables. One was Margaret Pierce, who was smoking a cigarette and sipping dolefully at a Coke. The other, a sleek brunette named Laura, was peering into a compact, adjusting her make-up. Regan poured herself a cup of coffee and joined them at the table.

'Lord, am I beat!' she exclaimed.

Margaret made a wry face. 'Aren't we all?'

Laura snapped her compact shut and slipped it into her jacket pocket. 'Well, how goes it with the great man?' she drawled. 'Any interesting little titbits of gossip about his love-life?'

Regan snorted decorously. 'Don't ask me. The only time he speaks to me is when he brings me another batch of documents to stamp or needs copies made.'

Laura laughed. 'Well, at least you don't have to worry about him making a pass at you.' She wrinkled her delicate turned-up nose. 'Not like some of the others I could mention. Although I'll have to admit

I wouldn't mind a try at him. What a dishy hunk of man!'

'Are we talking about the same person?' Regan enquired in a wry tone. 'Nick Wainwright?'

Laura snickered. 'You've got it. Too bad he's got this thing about fooling around with the women he works with. You know,' she added dreamily, 'it would almost be worth quitting just to get a shot at him. No future in it, of course, but what an experience!'

Regan wrinkled her nose, quite unable to share Laura's enthusiasm for the man's charms. 'Well, I guess there's no disputing tastes,' she commented drily. 'I'm afraid he doesn't do much for me along those lines.'

Laura rose from the table and smoothed down the skirt of her tight black suit. 'Well, duty calls. I'm drafting a brief for Jim Courtney, and as usual he wants it yesterday. I'll probably have to work the weekend, just when my boyfriend has finally managed to get a few days away from his wife.'

Regan commiserated with Laura on her bad luck, but made a mental note to try her best to avoid such complications.

When Laura was gone, Regan turned to Margaret, who had just lit a fresh cigarette and was concentrating hard on a legal document spread out before her on the table.

'You've been here for a few years now, Margaret,' she said, just to make conversation. 'When do they let you start practising real law?'

Margaret raised her eyes slowly from her papers and turned to give Regan a blank look. 'What do you mean?'

'Well, for three weeks now all I've done around here is unskilled labour that any moron off the street could probably do better. I'm really getting fed up with it. Do they treat all new lawyers like this or is it just me? Sometimes I think——'

'Oh, believe me, you're not a special case,' Margaret snapped. She stubbed her cigarette out in the ashtray. 'No matter what they say, it really is harder for a woman to make it in the professions.'

Regan was taken aback by the woman's curt tone. She knew that Margaret was married and had children. That must be a hard act to juggle, and something was obviously troubling her. It had been a tactical error to pour out her own troubles to her that way.

'Sorry,' she said stiffly. 'I didn't mean to ramble on like that.'

Margaret sighed. 'Oh, don't mind me,' she said in a more friendly tone. 'It's just that sometimes it all piles up. You know what I mean?'

Regan smiled. 'It sounds as though everyone must be overworked around here.'

'Oh, it's not that,' Margaret said with a shrug. 'I can handle the job. It's all the other things that get to me once in a while. I was up most of the night with my youngest, who tends to get ear infections easily.'

'How many children do you have?' Regan asked.

'Two,' Margaret replied, brightening. 'A boy and a girl.'

'It must be hard, trying to hold down a job and raise a family, keep up a home. How do you manage?'

Margaret smiled. 'Oh, I'll admit it gets hairy at times.' She spread her arms and lifted her shoulders.

'But what can you do? I love my job, and I love my husband and kids.'

'I guess you have to learn to be Superwoman,' Regan said with a little laugh.

'Well, that would help.' Margaret's eyes softened. 'But what it really takes is an understanding husband. I'm fortunate that mine respects my career and really pitches in at home to do his share. And, since we both have good jobs, we can afford to hire help.' She rose to her feet. 'Listen, Regan, don't let Old Nick get you down. He's the worst of the bunch, and you'll probably be rotated in time.'

Regan looked up at her. 'Do you think the gossip about his personal life is really true?'

'Who knows?' She grinned. 'At least it gives the rest of us something to talk about.'

When she was gone, Regan sat alone for a while drinking her coffee, thinking about Margaret's juggling act. It made her own problems seem pretty insignificant, but in a way she envied her. It would be nice to have it all, even if the cost was high.

She threw her empty cup in the waste-bin, and went back to her own office, past the elegant reception-room. She'd miss it here. Maybe she would be assigned to another partner. Surely not all male lawyers had Nick's chauvinistic attitude towards women.

When she reached her door she stopped short when she saw that the man himself was inside, perched on the edge of her desk and leafing through the memo she'd left in his office earlier. She was surprised to see him, but no longer quite so awed by him or anxious to please. She didn't care any more. She wished now she had written out her letter of resignation in final form, just so she'd have the satisfaction of seeing his face when she handed it to him in person.

He looked up at her. 'This is good work, McIntyre,' he said. He slid off the desk and came towards her.

For the first time since she'd known him, he was smiling, and Regan couldn't take her eyes off him. It transformed him utterly. The grey eyes glittered, the scowl lines on his forehead and around his mouth were smoothed out, and the thought flitted into her mind that now she could begin to see the reason for the gossip about him. He was a *very* attractive man.

'In fact,' he went on, 'it's damned good. Just what I wanted.' He tossed the memo down on her desk and started to walk past her. At the door, he turned back. 'By the way,' he remarked casually, 'there's going to be a meeting of co-counsel this afternoon in the large conference room. I want you to be there with me. Two o'clock sharp.'

When he was gone, Regan stood there for several long moments trying to assimilate what had just happened. A feeling of tingling excitement rose up within her. Her anger fled, her decision to quit her job was forgotten. He'd actually paid her a compliment! She could hardly believe it.

The important thing was that now, with just that small praise, the whole thing became worthwhile, even the stamping and the photocopying. She crossed over to her desk, took out the draft of her letter of resignation, tore it into tiny pieces and threw it in the wastebasket.

At a few minutes before two o'clock, Regan stood at the closed door to Nick's office waiting for him and hoping for a few minutes alone with him before the meeting. As usual, he'd left her totally in the dark as to what he expected her to do.

She had just raised her hand to knock, when the door was flung open and he stepped out into the hall, almost knocking her down.

'OK, McIntyre,' he said. 'Let's go.'

He forged on ahead of her, and she practically tripped trying to keep up with his long strides. Obviously he wasn't going to give her time to ask any questions. She'd just have to play it by ear and hope for the best.

The large conference room was located just off the reception area. It was enormous, forty feet long and half as wide, with a large bank of windows overlooking the city at the far end, and at the other a small alcove containing coffee and tea. In the centre was a long table with a hammered brass top. Around it were at least twenty chairs, most of them occupied.

The air was thick with tobacco smoke and noisy with the constant hum of conversation. Those who weren't seated at the table stood in small clusters beside it, absorbed in conversation, replete with gestures, as each group plotted its course of attack.

As host lawyer, Nick would sit at the head of the table, and Regan followed him there, hoping he meant her to sit next to him. Apparently he did, because, when he reached his chair, he nodded curtly at the one beside him before he sat down.

As those standing gradually began to shuffle towards their seats, he turned to Regan and bent his head close to hers. Oh, good, she thought, he's finally going to clue me in what the meeting is all about. She perked up her ears, ready to receive his words of wisdom.

'Will you see that everyone has coffee or tea?' he said in a low voice.

Regan's mouth fell open and the blood rushed into her face. She was about to object strenuously to his cavalier request, but he had already straightened up and turned to read through the papers set before him on the table. What should she do? What *could* she do? It wasn't in her to make a scene, and, if she refused, that's what would happen. She'd just have to bite the bullet and play waitress for him.

Slowly, she rose to her feet. As she did, she glanced down at his notes and saw that the memo she'd presented him with that morning was right on top. That was some consolation, but her cheeks still burned as she went around the table from person to person. At least she had the presence of mind not to offer to serve them. She merely told them what was available at the small serving counter and let them shift for themselves.

At last they were all seated around the table and looking expectantly at Nick.

'All right, everybody,' he said in a loud, commanding tone. 'Shall we get started?'

As the meeting progressed, Regan soon found that all she had to do was sit there with her mouth shut and listen. They were all too busy to pay any attention to her. It was really very instructive. There were strong arguments presented from all sides, sometimes escalating into acrimonious battles, and, even though she played no real part in the proceedings, it was thrilling to her to finally be able to participate in a real legal contest with the big boys, even at her menial level.

There were three other women present, who were several years older than Regan and seemed very experienced at this sort of thing. They managed to keep up, shout for shout, with the men, never giving ground, making their points firmly and with supreme self-confidence. As Regan watched them in action, her heart quailed. Would she ever be able to perform like that in a roomful of aggressive men?

Well, she'd darned well better, she told herself firmly. Why else had she made so many sacrifices and suffered through all those years of schooling? She was young, she could learn, and soon she became so deeply absorbed in watching how they conducted themselves that she didn't realise Nick was speaking to her until she felt him nudge her sharply with his elbow.

She turned to him expectantly, and was startled to see his face only inches away from hers. He leaned even closer, his mouth at her ear, his cheek almost touching hers. The voices of the others began to fade as she grew more intensely aware of the closeness of the man sitting beside her, the scent of his skin, the warmth of his body, the weight of his arm as it pressed against hers.

Out of the blue, the comments Laura had made about him that morning flashed into her mind. At the time she'd only laughed at the thought of calling Nick a 'dishy hunk of man'. Now, suddenly, she wasn't so sure.

Then she felt his warm breath in her ear, and a little shiver ran up and down her spine.

'What the hell are you doing?' he muttered.

She came back down to earth with a dull thud. 'I'm not doing anything,' she replied, bewildered.

'That's what I mean,' his voice ground on. 'For heaven's sake, can't you make yourself useful? Aren't you even taking notes?'

She jerked her head back and stared at him. They were still so close that she could see the dark stubble on his jaw, the angry little pulse beating just below his ear. For a brief second, their eyes met and locked together. Then, to her amazement, a light flush washed over his face and he looked away.

'Here,' he muttered, sliding some papers towards her. 'Go make twenty copies of this document, then pass it around when you come back.'

She snatched angrily at the papers and stalked out into the hall. At the photocopier in the workroom, she stood there while the machine cranked out the copies, still simmering with humiliation and fury. That brief moment when his head had bent to hers, along with the strange sensations it had aroused in her, was completely forgotten.

When she got back to the conference-room the meeting seemed to be breaking up. Hurriedly, she passed out the copies she'd just made, then went to the head of the table to receive further orders, half inclined to give him a smart salute.

Nick was involved in a conversation with a young man about her own age, and, as she stood there waiting, Regan couldn't help noticing how Nick interacted with him, so differently from the way he treated her. He was listening attentively, one hand rubbing along his jaw, a bemused expression on his face. At one point, when he threw back his head and roared with laughter, Regan could hardly believe her eyes. She'd never seen him laugh, never even thought he knew how.

When the others began to drift out of the room, Regan went to the window and stood looking out at the rain, waiting for the axe to fall. He was obviously disappointed in her performance today, and she had to admit that she probably should have figured it out for herself that he'd want her to take notes.

Nick had walked out to the lifts with the others, and now Regan could hear his footsteps coming back. Then there was dead silence in the room. She turned around to see him walking towards her, a grim look on his face. She raised her chin and waited. When he came within a few feet of her, he stopped short, rested his knuckles on his lean hips and glared coldly at her.

'Well,' he drawled at last. 'You were a big help.'

CHAPTER THREE

REGAN simply saw red. 'And just what was it you wanted me to do?' she demanded angrily. 'Serve the coffee myself? Perhaps I should bring an apron to work from now on, a little frilly one, with a matching cap. Or should I have brought that damned stamping machine?' She made a sweeping gesture with her arms and raised her voice to a dramatic pitch. 'I do make nice copies, though. Isn't that what you pay me for? Or maybe you expected me to get up and do a dance on the table. Is that it?'

Nick Wainwright's eyes had narrowed into slits by now and she could actually *hear* his laboured breathing. She knew she'd gone too far, that he was literally beside himself with fury, but by now she couldn't care less. He'd humiliated her in front of the others, treated her like a drudge, criticised her, ignored her, shown her in every possible way that he didn't want her there at all. She had nothing to lose.

Their eyes locked together in a silent contest of wills. Regan was determined not to back down if she had to stand there throughout all eternity facing him down.

Suddenly she became aware that his mouth was twitching, the black look was fading, and in the next moment he was grinning broadly at her.

The smile lit up his face. The white teeth flashed against his rather tanned skin, the grey eyes had lost their cold, stony hue, and she noticed for the first time that there were bright flecks of a darker colour in the pupils.

'OK, McIntyre,' he said at last. 'You win. I guess I've treated you unfairly right from the beginning.'

'I can't argue with that,' she said, still seething.

He cocked his head to one side. 'Maybe I was testing you. Did you ever think of that?'

'Not really.'

'Actually, it was clear to me quite early on that you had what it takes. Those memos you kept sending me demonstrated your ability to get right to the heart of the matter, the most essential quality in the successful practice of law. What I still needed to find out was whether you had any spunk.' He nodded appreciatively. 'Now that you've shown a little, I'm willing to admit that you just might have the makings of a good lawyer.'

'You are?' she asked.

He slapped her heartily on the back, almost knocking her off her feet. 'Damned right.' Then he held up a warning hand. 'But don't get carried away with it. I won't stand for insubordination. You can argue with me if you've got a point to make, but don't ever forget that I'm the boss.'

It was on the tip of her tongue to assure him smartly that there was no danger of that, given his monumental ego, but prudence won out in the end and she held her tongue.

'Fair enough,' she said.

'Now,' he said, all business again, 'I have to fly to San Francisco on Sunday for a meeting of co-counsel to finish up last-minute details before we go to trial. I'll need a dogsbody and I want you to come with me.'

Regan's heart soared. At last! And this time she'd make sure she pinned him down to detailed instructions beforehand. Forcing herself to remain calm, she nodded. 'All right,' she said.

'We'll leave Sunday night. Check with Sheila about the flight number and departure time. We'll meet at the airport and I'll fill in the details on the trip down.' His eyes flicked over her. 'And since we'll only be gone a week, don't pack your entire wardrobe.' He glanced at his watch. 'It's past five o'clock. And Friday night, at that. I'm leaving now. You might as well go home, too.'

With a little wave, he turned and walked out of the room. Regan could hardly believe things had turned out this way. She'd thought for sure he'd fire her after her outburst. Instead he'd apologised! Well, almost. Probably as close to an apology as he'd ever come.

He only wanted a dogsbody, he'd said, and it would only be for a week, but, if she did a good job, he might want her with him during the trial. Suddenly she had a strong urge to call her father. This time she had good news for him.

Regan was so excited about the trip that she spent the entire weekend dithering around her apartment, jumping from one task to another. In the middle of writing a note to the postman, she suddenly *had* to iron a blouse. She washed her hair three times, trying to decide which style made her look the most professional, and changed her mind a dozen times about whether to defrost the refrigerator.

The only damper on her high spirits was her father's reaction to the news. She'd called him as soon as she got home on Friday night, still almost incoherent with joy. But when she'd told him about the trip, there had been a long silence on the line.

When it had stretched on for what seemed like a full minute, she'd begun to think they'd been cut off. He lived in a rural area on the outskirts of Yakima, a small farming community in the eastern part of the state that still wasn't blessed with the most up-to-date telephone equipment.

'Dad, are you still there?' she'd finally asked.

'Yes, honey. I'm here,' came her father's slow reply.

'Well, did you hear what I said? Nick Wainwright is going to take me with him to an important meeting in San Francisco on the pharmaceutical case I told you about.'

'I heard you.' There was another short silence. 'This boss of yours,' he said then. 'What's he like?'

Then it dawned on her. He was worried about her travelling alone with a man! If it hadn't been so pathetic, it would have been funny.

Her father was still living in the Dark Ages as far as his three daughters were concerned. Regan had lived away from the town she'd grown up in for so many years that she'd forgotten how hidebound he could be, how Victorian his sense of what was proper for a young single woman.

Her two sisters had married young and still lived in Yakima not far from the family home. They had nice safe husbands and were well settled as far as he was concerned. But Regan was the baby, the clever one, and he'd always treated her like the son he'd never had, especially after her mother had died when she was only twelve.

It really wasn't fair. He was the one who had encouraged her to be independent, urged her to go on to law school when she'd finished college, to make her way in a man's world. Now, just when she got her first big chance to prove herself in her profession, he was playing the heavy father and asking what kind of man her boss was. If he only knew!

Then she did laugh. 'Dad, I couldn't be more safe with you than I'll be with Nick Wainwright.'

Obviously not impressed, he only asked, 'How old is this man?'

She'd just looked it up last week. 'He's thirty-seven.'

'Is he married?'

'Well, no, but that doesn't make any difference.'

It was on the tip of her tongue to tell him that, in her experience, marriage didn't necessarily keep a man from straying, but decided that wouldn't be very reassuring news to him.

'I mean,' she hastened to add, 'that he has a firm rule never to get involved with a woman he works with. Not only that, but he actively resists working with women at all. As a matter of fact, I wouldn't have been hired in the first place if our managing partner hadn't forced him into it. That's why this trip is such a plum for me.'

'Well, if you say so,' her father said grudgingly. 'But be careful, honey. It's a wicked world, and I wouldn't want you to get carried away and do anything silly that might ruin your career. You're a very beautiful girl, you know.' Then he chuckled. 'And you know what men are like.'

After she had reassured him several times that she was well aware of all the dangers in his 'wicked world', that she really was capable of taking care of herself, and that she'd call him as soon as she got home the following Friday, they hung up.

Thinking about that conversation on Sunday morning while she was in her bedroom finishing her packing, Regan couldn't help smiling at her father's opinion of her physical charms. Somehow he had it firmly fixed in his mind that his youngest daughter was a raving beauty who spent half her life fending off amorous advances from hordes of men, all panting to seduce her.

It was almost funny, since actually nothing could be further from the truth. She glanced up from her packing to glance at her reflection in the bedroom mirror. What she saw was a slim, tallish young woman with light brown hair cut shoulder-length and tucked behind her ears, nice brown eyes that were clear and direct, but with no trace of seductive power that she could make out, and dressed in faded jeans and an old flannel shirt.

She had a decent bone-structure and a passable figure that wore clothes well, but she was certainly no beauty and as far as she knew had never inflamed a man's lust, except for some adolescent pawing during her schooldays.

At any rate, not a man like Nick Wainwright. If office gossip was anywhere near the truth, his taste in women ran to a more flamboyant type, like models or young society debs, and there were even rumours of a semi-famous actress who had been in Seattle a few years back making a film. Her poor father had nothing to worry about on that score.

Regan sighed a little regretfully, ran a hand through her smooth hair, then turned back to her packing. She planned to wear her dark blue suit on the plane and had carefully folded her grey flannel suit in her bag, along with an extra jacket, several clean blouses and changes of underwear.

She'd been debating all weekend whether to take along a dressier outfit, just in case. She had no idea what the protocol might be on these occasions. Would Nick expect her to go out to dinner with him in the evening? Or did he intend to stick her in some dingy closet of a hotel room stamping documents and making lists night and day?

Actually, she didn't own a suitable dress for evening wear anyway, and, since her small suitcase was already full, in the end she decided to go with the strictly businesslike clothes she'd already packed.

The flight was scheduled to take off at seven-fifteen on Sunday night. Regan had intended to drive her battered Volkswagen to the airport car park and leave it there while she was gone, but at the last minute Don Jameson, a young man who lived in the apartment directly above hers, offered to drive her.

She had gone upstairs to let him know she would be gone for a week, give him an extra key, and ask him to keep an eye on her place for her.

She'd only lived in the apartment for six months, and didn't know any other neighbours. Don was a pleasant, fresh-faced young intern at the University Hospital, who had unruly sandy-coloured hair and wore a perpetual friendly grin on his boyish face. Their first encounter had been a complaint from Regan about the loud rock music he played at all hours of the night.

When she'd finally complained, fed up at last with being awakened at all hours by the steady, pounding beat—he seemed to be particularly fond of bass notes—he'd apologised so profusely and afterwards been so good about keeping it down, that they'd become friends, occasionally sharing a pizza or going out for hamburgers together.

Now, when he answered his door and she told him what she wanted, he agreed immediately and then insisted on driving her to the airport. Before she could argue, he'd got his wallet and car keys and was out in the hall beside her. They went down to his car, parked in front of the kerb, and he stowed her suitcase in the back.

'This is very nice of you, Don,' she said as he got inside and started the engine. 'You're a real life-saver. At the last minute I decided I'd better defrost my refrigerator, and by the time I finished it was already six-thirty. I was beginning to panic that I might miss my flight.'

'Off on a wild week of sinful pleasure?' he asked playfully as he whizzed through the Sunday evening traffic.

'Hardly,' she replied with a laugh. 'It's a business trip.'

'I'm impressed.'

'If you knew my boss, you wouldn't be,' she replied drily. 'I'm supposed to meet him at the airport, and he's a stickler for punctuality.'

'Well, this will save you a little time, anyway,' Don said, narrowly missing a parked car as he swerved around to the right to pass a truck. 'When are you coming back? I can pick you up if I'm not on call at the hospital.'

'Friday night,' she replied, hanging on to her seat for dear life. 'I'm not sure what time.'

'Well, call me when you get in.'

They finally made their way out of the congested downtown traffic and reached the motorway. From then on it was smooth sailing, and, in just a few minutes, Don had pulled up in front of the airline terminal. Regan glanced at her watch. Thanks to Don's daredevil driving, they'd made the trip in just under twenty minutes. She wouldn't be late, after all.

'Don't get out, Don,' she said as she opened her door. 'I only have the one suitcase and can manage it myself.'

She stepped out on to the pavement, then reached in the back to retrieve her bag. She set it down and leaned over at the open car window to say goodbye to Don.

'Have a good trip,' he said cheerfully. 'And do call me Friday night. As far as I know I'll be free.'

'Thanks again, Don. I really appreciate this.'

With a little salute, he gunned the engine and tore off down the sloping driveway back towards the motorway.

Regan still had to find Nick, who presumably had their tickets. She had no idea where to look for him, and wished he'd been a little more specific. All he'd said was that he'd meet her at the airport, which covered an awful lot of territory. If she had to spend a lot of time looking for him, it would make her even later, and she began to panic again.

Frantic now to get inside and start searching for him, she had just picked up her bag and turned towards the entrance, when he simply appeared before her eyes. He was standing in front of the glass doors, his arms folded across his chest, watching her, a faint mocking smile on his lips. Apparently he'd been there all the time.

She hurried towards him. 'I'm sorry I'm so late,' she said breathlessly.

'Out joyriding with the boyfriend?' he drawled.

'No,' she stammered. 'No, it wasn't like that. You see, I had to defrost the refrigerator and didn't realise——'

'Spare me the gory details,' he broke in with an exasperated sigh. 'Let's get moving now, or we'll both miss the plane.'

It was a short flight, only an hour and fifteen minutes, hardly time for Nick to fill her in completely on the meetings they were to attend, and once they were air-borne Regan turned to him expectantly, eager to hear the pearls of wisdom drop from his lips.

'I'm going to have a drink,' he announced. 'How about you?'

It wasn't at all what she had expected. 'Well, I don't know,' she faltered. 'I'm not much of a drinker.'

The stewardess, a striking and very curvaceous young blonde, had come to hover over them and was gazing down at Nick with limpid blue eyes. Regan glanced at him. There was no mistaking the gleam in those grey eyes as they expertly swept over the blonde.

Regan had never seen that look before. It was so smoothly and unobtrusively done as to be hardly noticeable to a casual observer. She glanced up at the blonde. *She* had obviously noticed it. The warm, inviting smile on her full pouty lips was clearly an invitation.

For some reason Regan found this suggestive little interplay extremely annoying. They were on a business trip, for heaven's sake! Couldn't he keep his libido under control long enough to discuss the case with her?

As though he'd read her mind, Nick's head came around and he gave her an impatient look. No invitation there! She lowered her eyes, embarrassed to be caught staring.

'Well, McIntyre?' he snapped. 'Do you want a drink or don't you?'

'No,' she said curtly, and turned her head to gaze out of the window.

It was a bright, clear evening in mid June, and the sun was still shining above a thin layer of clouds. Regan loved to fly, and it had been a long time since she'd been on an aeroplane. She dreamed of some day going somewhere really exciting. She'd never been to Europe, or South America, actually had never seen much of her own country except the West Coast.

Then she heard the clink of ice cubes next to her and a long swallow. Nick had obviously been served his drink, and she turned back to him. He looked contented and quite pleased with himself.

'You said you'd fill me in about the meetings on the way down,' she said with a touch of frost in her voice.

'Right,' he replied.

He proceeded to explain in short concise sentences that they were to meet with lawyers for the other plaintiffs in the case to discuss strategy for the up-coming trial and compare notes on the documents each had inspected so far.

This took all of five minutes, and at the end of it he reached into his briefcase and pulled out a thick manila folder.

'Here,' he said, handing it to her. 'Read this. It's a summary of what's been agreed on so far. I'm going to catch forty winks.'

Then, to her amazement, he snapped his briefcase shut, settled his head back on the seat and closed his eyes.

Regan felt like slapping him. That was some explanation! She made a face at him, hoping his eyes really were shut all the way. Then, when he didn't stir, she gave him a closer look.

Funny how different his face appeared in repose. Awake, his expressions were volatile, changing from impatience to serious business to that maddening mocking smile, even to frankly suggestive, as in the case of the blonde stewardess, in a matter of seconds.

His eyelashes were awfully long for a man, she thought, and coal-black, as were the heavy eyebrows, but she still considered that fine straight nose his best feature. She glanced down at his hands, which were still holding his empty glass loosely in his lap. They were large, capable hands, with long tapering fingers and covered on the backs with a sprinkling of sleek dark hair.

Yet he wasn't story-book handsome, nor was it actually his looks that made him so appealing to women. It was more the sense of taut power, of reserves of emotional energy held in check, but which could erupt at any moment in anger, scathing criticism—or desire.

He shifted slightly in his seat just then, so that his knee touched hers. It was like a current of electricity, astounding in its power to shake her, and suddenly it dawned on her just where her idle thoughts had taken her. She was supposed to be angry with him!

Quickly, she tore her eyes away from the sleeping man, and started poring over the documents he had given her. Soon she became totally absorbed in the intricacies of the case, and it wasn't until they were flying over the shining white peak of Mount Shasta in northern California that she realised he was awake. In fact, out of the corner of her eye she could see that he was staring at her intently.

She turned to him, and was surprised to see an expression of genuine amusement on his face. The drink and the nap seemed to have mellowed him considerably. Or maybe he'd been daydreaming about the blonde stewardess. Finally she gave him an enquiring look, and he began to chuckle under his breath.

'I was just thinking,' he explained, 'about your offer Friday afternoon to dance on the table. Somehow I can't quite picture that, although it might be interesting. What did you have in mind for a costume? Feathers? Balloons? Bubbles?'

She flushed deeply and dropped her eyes. 'I was only being facetious,' she mumbled.

He continued to eye her speculatively, chin in hand. 'Actually, it wouldn't hurt to wear something a little more feminine once in a while than that crisp little uniform of yours.'

Regan eyed him suspiciously. This from a man who believed women had no place in a man's profession? 'I thought it was the fact that I'm female that turned you against me in the first place.'

'Listen,' he said in a confidential tone. 'The law is a game. You need to learn the rules and play within them, but the object is to win. One of the reasons I don't like working with women is that they can throw a man off base when they start using the little feminine tricks they seem to learn in the cradle. I've seen strong men reduced to gibbering idiots at the sight of a woman's tears, or a certain way of batting her eyes.'

'I'm sorry,' she said stiffly. 'I don't operate that way.'

He shrugged. 'If you've got it, flaunt it.'

'And dance on the table,' she stated indignantly.

'Now you're only being obstructive. I'm not talking about sex. I'm only saying that most men are putty in the hands of a truly feminine woman. A clever girl can play a man's game and still win a point or two just by acting like a woman.'

'I haven't the slightest idea what you're talking about,' she commented flatly.

He raised a quizzical eyebrow. 'I think you do, McIntyre. And if you really don't, then you'd better learn.'

Just then the captain's voice came over the loudspeaker, telling the passengers that they would be landing in five minutes, to fasten seatbelts, and thanking them for flying United.

When they arrived at the San Francisco airport, they went directly to the rental office, where Sheila had arranged to have a car waiting for them. Nick drove skilfully, not taking any chances, but not lagging behind either, and as though he knew the city well.

All along the way, he was strangely silent. Regan assumed that he was concentrating on his driving, but occasionally, when they were stopped at a traffic light, she could have sworn he was darting her brief sidelong glances. She was so thrilled at the adventure she was having, however, that she didn't pay attention to it, and continued to goggle out of the window at the city sights, the Golden Gate Bridge in the background, the steep hills of the city, the tall buildings.

When they pulled into the curving drive in front of the hotel, they left the car with the valet service, and went inside to register. At the desk, the moment the clerk looked up and saw Nick, his face lit up with a broad welcoming smile.

'Ah, Mr Wainwright,' he burbled. 'How nice to have you with us again.'

While the two men exchanged pleasantries, Regan looked around the elegant lobby with a heady feeling of excitement, basking in the glow of the attention Nick was getting. Obviously, he was well-known here, at one of San Francisco's finest hotels, and an important and valued guest. She stood there, watching all the bustle and activity on their behalf.

The clerk turned the register around, then punched the bell on the desk while Nick signed in. A uniformed bellboy appeared out of nowhere and began to stack their luggage on a cart. When Nick had completed his business, the clerk thanked him profusely, wished him a pleasant stay, and beckoned to the boy.

'Mr Wainwright will be in his usual suite,' he said, handing him a key.

Suite? Regan stared at him. What did he mean by that? She came down to earth with a dull thud. She glanced around in total confusion. By now, Nick and the boy with their bags had walked off and were already halfway to the lift. All she could think of to do was scurry after them.

The lift was crowded, and Regan was pressed further back in the corner at each floor. The ride seemed endless. She couldn't move, could scarcely breathe. But she could think. And the thoughts racing through her head were not reassuring.

She'd been so excited at the unexpected chance to make this trip with Nick, so pleased that he seemed finally to be treating her as a lawyer, that the one possibility she'd never considered was that he had an ulterior motive. Now that it was probably too late, she began to have serious doubts.

One recollection after another tumbled into her mind—her father's warnings, the strange looks Nick had given her in the car, the conversation on the plane. Just what had he been suggesting with his comments about her clothes—her 'uniform' as he called it—and about using her femininity?

In fact, during that conversation there had been a gleam in those grey eyes that was unpleasantly familiar to her, somehow reminded her of the passes she'd had to fend off from over-amorous dates during her college years.

Those things, combined with the memory of the gossip in the coffee-room about his reputation with women, now made her wonder if what he had had in mind with his advice was that sleeping with him would further her career. No, it couldn't be. Or could it?

She was jolted out of her reverie by a sharp tug at her arm. She snapped out of it to see Nick frowning at her.

'Come on, McIntyre,' he said. 'This is our floor.'

Still in a daze, she straggled after Nick and the bellboy until they came to a door in the middle of the corridor. The boy unlocked it, then stepped aside while Nick went in. Regan hesitated, but when Nick turned around and glared at her over his shoulder she followed him. What else could she do at this point?

The room she found herself in was pleasant, but not ostentatious. There were some comfortable-looking chairs, a sturdy desk against one wall, and in the middle of the room a large table on top of which were several sealed cardboard cartons. Nick placed his briefcase on the table and immediately took command.

He directed the boy where to put each bag, saw him to the door, took charge of the key and tipped him, while Regan stood in the middle of the room and waited, her heart in her throat. This was one situation that hadn't been covered in law school, and she dreaded the possibility of a scene.

When the boy was gone, and she was alone with Nick, her head began to clear, and she could feel the first faint stirrings of anger. She wasn't a prisoner, after all. What could he do to her? Even assuming he had set her up, lured her to go off with him with a lie about a business trip, when all he had in mind was a seduction, she was not a helpless young girl.

As her anger grew, so did her courage. She turned around to face him. He was at the table opening one of the cartons and sorting through its contents, a look of intense concentration on his face. Regan walked over to his side. He didn't acknowledge her presence by so much as a glance in her direction.

'Nick,' she said in a loud voice.

'Just a minute, McIntyre,' he muttered. 'Can't you see I'm busy?'

Then she began to have doubts about the conclusions she'd jumped to. He certainly wasn't treating her like a woman he had plans to talk into bed. Maybe she was wrong. Still, she had to find out.

Finally he finished what he was doing and turned to her. 'Yes?' he said. 'What is it?'

'About this suite,' she began.

'What about it?'

'Well, I'm rather surprised, that's all,' she faltered, and when she saw the distant frosty look on his face, words failed her altogether. It was about as far from desire as one could imagine, and she deeply regretted having raised the subject at all.

'Come on, McIntyre,' he said at last with an impatient wave of his hand. 'If you've got something on your mind, spit it out. We have work to do.'

She opened her mouth, but nothing came out.

Then a light seemed to dawn in his eyes and he looked down that fine patrician nose at her with a mocking smile. 'Ah,' he said. 'I see. It's the suite that's bothering you, isn't it? You were expecting to have your own virginal little room.'

By this time, Regan felt very hot, and knew her face must be crimson. She looked down at her feet. 'Well, as I say, I'm just surprised.'

He leaned his hips back on the table, folded his arms over his chest and gave her a scathing look. For her part, Regan was wishing the floor would open up and swallow her at that point.

'Well, I admit we have to share a connecting bathroom,' he drawled sarcastically. 'But I'm very neat. There are also solid locks on both doors. I intend to use mine, and I suggest you do the same.' Then his gaze hardened. 'Let's get one thing straight right now,' he went on stonily. 'I have nothing against love nests or amorous adventures. I'm not a monk. But I never—repeat, *never*—under any circumstances whatsoever get involved with a woman I work with. Is that clear?'

She nodded miserably.

'Believe me, you have nothing to fear from me. As far as this trip is concerned, you're only another lawyer, not a woman at all. Understood?'

She nodded again. She prayed he was through with his tirade, but apparently he was having such a good time at her expense he had no intention of letting her off the hook quite so easily. He was growing expansive now, pacing around the room in long strides, just as though he was performing in a courtroom and she was the witness wriggling on the stand.

'Let me ask you a hypothetical question. If you were a man—which you apparently have ambitions to be—and since we'll be working late often, wouldn't you accept it as perfectly natural that we'd stay in a suite together, simply for the sake of convenience?'

'Yes,' she said in a small voice. 'I guess so.'

He nodded, apparently satisfied at last. 'Just keep in mind that you're here for one purpose, and that's to work. And you can start by sorting those documents on the table into chronological order. I'm going to take a shower.'

He strode away from her, but when he reached the door, he stopped and called back to her. 'One more thing, McIntyre.'

She sighed and turned around to face him. 'Yes, sir.'

He was smiling, but it wasn't pleasant. 'If I want *feminine* companionship, I can find it quite easily elsewhere.'

'I'll just bet,' she muttered under her breath, but by then he was gone, and she turned back to start on the documents.

CHAPTER FOUR

REGAN was awakened the next morning by the sound of water running in the adjoining bathroom. She'd lived alone for so long that it startled her at first, and she couldn't think where she was. She'd slept like the dead, worn out both from the excitement of the trip and from having worked on sorting documents until almost midnight.

She was still half asleep when it dawned on her that the noise coming from next door must be Nick in the shower, and a sudden fleeting vision of the man himself, standing under the spray, lathering himself, flashed into her mind. It was gone as quickly as it came, however, and, fully awake by now, she jumped out of bed and ran to the window.

The city was barely stirring at that hour of the morning, only six-thirty by her watch, and there was a thin haze of fog obscuring the view of the street below. But even through the double-glazed windows she could hear the muffled clang of the cable cars just a few blocks away, the rumble of a truck rolling by, and, from the bay, the low groan of a foghorn.

The shower was suddenly shut off in the bathroom, and a few minutes later she heard a click as the lock on her door was undone. Assuming that meant he was finished in there and it was now her turn, she gathered up her toilet articles and cautiously opened the door a crack. She was met with a burst of warm steam, but other than that the room was empty.

She slipped inside, laid her belongings on the counter top and immediately stepped over to lock the door on Nick's side. Back at the counter, she noticed that he had wiped the mirror dry and hung his wet towel neatly on the rack. The steam was evaporating, but there was still a lingering scent in the air, an unmistakable masculine aroma of soap and a mild lemony aftershave.

It wasn't until after she'd had her shower, dried off and brushed her teeth that she noticed the brown leather toiletry case at the far end of the counter. It was unzipped. She gazed at it for a few minutes, debating, then her curiosity got the better of her. With a sense of daring, she cautiously nudged the edges apart with the back of her hand, as though afraid of leaving fingerprints, and peered inside.

There was shaving gear, a squat bottle of expensive-looking aftershave, a plastic soap dish, toothpaste, a toothbrush in a holder—and by then she began to feel guilty for snooping around in his personal things. Besides, the sight of all that masculine paraphernalia unnerved her. She felt a strange quickening of her pulse, an unsettling feeling of warmth.

She hung up her own towel and gathered her things together. Before going back into her bedroom, she remembered to unlock the door on Nick's side.

When she had dressed in her grey flannel suit, silk shirt and sensible shoes, she walked slowly out into the main room. Nick was already there, standing at the large table in the centre with his back towards her. He was in his shirt-sleeves, his hands braced on the table, leaning over to inspect the documents she'd arranged last night.

Regan stood in the doorway staring at him. It seemed so odd to her to see a man first thing in the morning. She felt shy, unsure quite how to approach him.

Finally she cleared her throat and said, 'Good morning.'

He picked up a file and held it up. 'This is the material we'll be using today,' he said with the merest backward glance in her direction. 'You can carry it in your briefcase.'

She went quickly to his side, took the file from him and glanced through it. Then for the next half-hour they discussed the case. At eight o'clock he put on his jacket.

'We'll go down for breakfast now. We're due at the meeting at nine o'clock, and you'd better take everything you need because we won't be coming back beforehand.'

Regan was too nervous to eat much breakfast, but she did manage to choke down a glass of orange juice, freshly squeezed now that they were in California, a half piece of toast and two cups of coffee. Nick tucked into an enormous meal of eggs and bacon, then topped it off with a stack of pancakes.

Watching him, Regan wondered where in the world he put it all. There wasn't an ounce of fat on his lean, lithe frame. He probably burned it off with all that quick energy, she decided. Even when he was sitting still, he gave the impression of being in perpetual motion.

Between bites, they continued to discuss the case, and when he'd finished off his last pancake and swallowed the last cup of coffee he signalled the waiter for the bill, signed it and rose to his feet.

All the meetings were to be held at the law offices of one of the firm's co-counsels, which was only a short walk from their hotel. By now, the morning traffic had picked up, and the city was bustling with office workers and shopkeepers on their way to work.

San Francisco was balmy in June, in spite of the perennial morning fogs, and even though Regan almost had to run to keep up with Nick's long strides she was thrilled to the very core of her being to be here at his side, walking along the streets of one of the most exciting cities in the world, on her way to a meeting that could very well have momentous impact on the business world.

All along the way, Nick kept up a running commentary on the imminent meeting, filling her in on personalities now, and giving her more specific instructions on what he expected of her than he'd ever bothered with before.

'I want you by my side taking notes,' he explained briskly. 'That's the most important thing, and it includes your impressions as well as the facts you learn. A lawyer's instincts are as important as his knowledge of the law, and it's never too soon to start developing them.'

She nodded eagerly. 'I understand,' she said, hoping she really did.

At the entrance to the building, he stopped to buy a *Wall Street Journal* at the stand out in front. He glanced through the first few pages, then handed it to her.

'Here,' he said. 'You keep this. Read it during the breaks.' He gave her a stern look. 'One more thing, McIntyre. If I ask you to have copies made or to get me a cup of coffee, try not to throw a tantrum. It's not because you're a woman, but because you're only a greenhorn who's expected to put in his—or her— time doing menial chores.'

She would have agreed to anything at that point, and she nodded again. 'OK. Understood.'

Then he smiled. 'And don't let the big boys scare you,' he said in a much gentler tone. 'Just remember that I chose you as part of my team, and you have every right to be there. Now, let's get going. We've got some tough battles ahead of us.'

At that moment, Regan would have followed him into hell itself. Just those few kind words were all it took to complete her happiness.

For the next few days Regan was so caught up in the excitement of the city and so fascinated by the operations of some of the best legal minds in the country that her initial reservations about sharing a suite with Nick now seemed like a distant childish dream.

For one thing, he kept her too busy even to think about anything but the job at hand. That Monday set the pattern for the next three days: up early, breakfast, go to meetings that lasted all day, with short breaks for lunch, a quick dinner at the hotel, usually with other lawyers present, then a long evening of work back in the suite, which by now had been turned into an office.

On Wednesday, at the noon break, as the others drifted out of the conference-room into the corridor, she stayed behind for a few moments to prepare for the afternoon session before leaving for lunch. Nick was at the door, involved in a conversation with one of the others, and when he was through he came back to speak to her alone.

'Good news,' he said brusquely. 'You've got the rest of the day off. Dick Carpenter has to fly to Los Angeles this afternoon and won't be back until late tonight. This will give you a chance to take in some of the sights.'

'Oh,' she said, and her face fell.

'You don't sound too thrilled,' he commented drily.

The truth was that she had no idea what to do with herself. More to the point, she couldn't help wondering what *he* would be doing. She had grown so used to being constantly with him that she felt a little lost at the prospect of several hours on her own.

'Oh, I am,' she said quickly. 'I was just thinking that if you need my help, I'd be glad to stick around.'

He shook his head and grinned at her. 'No, thanks. I have other plans.' He started to walk away from her, but turned back before he had gone more than a few steps. 'By the way,' he said. 'I almost forgot. There's to be a dinner party tonight at Joe Lombardi's house, and, since he's the head man in this firm, it's a command performance. Seven o'clock. I probably won't see you again, so I'll give you the address now. You can take a taxi. Put it on your expense account.'

He scribbled the address on her notepad, then turned and with a backward wave of his hand strode out of the room.

She stood there for a long time, then abstractedly began collecting her notes and stuffing them into the briefcase. What other plans did he have? she wondered. Of course, she knew quite well, just from that silly smirk on his face, that they must include female companionship. Well, what did she care? She wasn't interested in his personal life.

All the others had gone on ahead, apparently to take full advantage of the afternoon's reprieve, and she wandered out into the empty corridor by herself, lugging the full briefcase, and wondering what in the world she was going to do until seven o'clock.

When she got back to the hotel, the suite seemed strangely empty. It was the first time she'd been alone in it, and without Nick's dynamic presence she felt quite lost. After she had emptied the briefcase and inserted its contents in their proper place on the table, she decided she might as well take a nap, for lack of anything better to do.

On the way to her bedroom, a wicked impulse seized her, and she found herself almost without thinking, going the few steps out of her way that led past Nick's bedroom. The door was open. She wouldn't be prying exactly. She was only curious. Standing on tiptoe, she peeked inside.

As he'd said, he was very neat. The way he picked up after himself in the bathroom had already proved that. The bed had been made up by the maid in their absence, and the only personal objects she could see were his open suitcase on the floor and a set of brushes on the dresser.

The man was an enigma. She knew quite well he *had* a personal life, most likely a very colourful one, but you'd never know it from the pristine, almost monk-like state of his bedroom.

Yet he'd said he wasn't a monk. How she'd love to penetrate that reserve of his! The way he kept his professional and personal lives so completely separate was nothing short of Herculean. No one else she knew could accomplish that so completely. She thought of Margaret and her heroic efforts to juggle family and work. And Laura's long discussions about her rocky affair with a married man.

Was it just women who had trouble keeping the different areas of their lives compartmentalised? She'd heard the young male lawyers complaining about mortgages and instalment payments, or discussing the cars and houses they wanted to buy, but they rarely discussed their spouses or sweethearts or children the way the women did.

She went into her bedroom, kicked her shoes off and lay down on top of the bed. But she couldn't sleep. Something was nagging at the back of her mind, and after about ten agitated minutes she finally realised what was bothering her was the thought of the dinner party Nick had mentioned. She simply didn't want to go, not alone. Would he be angry if she didn't show up? Was it part of her job to attend social functions?

Finally she did doze off, but only for half an hour or so. What wakened her was her stomach growling. She'd had her usual half piece of toast for breakfast and no lunch yet. She glanced at her watch. It was past two o'clock. No wonder she was so starved.

She got off the bed, put on her shoes and went into the bathroom to wash her face and comb her hair. As she gazed at her reflection in the mirror, it suddenly dawned on her why she didn't want to go to that party. She looked like a drab little mouse who'd never been to a party in her life.

Suddenly she recalled Nick's nasty comments about the way she dressed on the plane trip down from Seattle on Sunday. She peered more closely in the mirror. Was she hopeless? No, she decided. There was a decent enough foundation there. What it needed was a little trimming.

Her spirits began to rise as she made her plans. She had the afternoon off. There was plenty of time to get her hair done and buy a new dress. Who knew? She might even have a good time tonight, and possibly even make Nick Wainwright eat his words.

At seven o'clock on the dot that evening, Regan's taxi pulled up in front of an imposing-looking house in an exclusive residential section situated high atop one of San Francisco's steep hills. It was a pleasant evening, and still light out, with a slight, gentle breeze blowing off the bay.

When she stepped out of the cab and looked up at the large sprawling pink stucco structure, the sloping red-tiled roof, the manicured garden in front, her nerve almost failed her. It looked more like a Spanish castle than a private residence.

Resisting the urge to jump back inside the cab and get back to the safety of the hotel, she paid the cabbie and watched him drive off. Then she pulled her new stole more tightly around her shoulders and started walking slowly up the wide curved brick steps to the heavy carved wooden door at the entrance.

As she rang the bell, she began to feel rather like an impostor, as though she were impersonating someone else. The dress that had seemed so irresistible that afternoon when she'd bought it now made her feel overdressed and half-naked at the same time. It was made of a heavy rust-coloured silk brocade, the square-necked bodice cut much lower than she was used to, and, she was afraid, revealing a little too much cleavage.

The new hairstyle felt strange, too. The unaccustomed curls at the top of her head and the fringe over her forehead were so stiff with spray that they felt glued on, as though they didn't really belong to her. She'd even had a professional make-up job, and although she'd insisted on a light application it still seemed she was hiding behind a mask.

Just then the door was opened. On the other side, peering out at her, stood a rather dashing dark-haired young man. When his eyes widened in a long appreciative gaze, Regan clutched the stole more tightly over her chest.

'Good evening,' she said. 'I'm Regan McIntyre.'

The young man grinned broadly and pulled the door open wide. 'Welcome, Megan,' he said. 'I'm the wastrel son of the house, Jack Lombardi.'

'It's *Regan*,' she explained as she stepped inside, stressing the R in her name. 'Not Megan.'

He waved a hand nonchalantly in the air. 'Whatever. "A rose by any other name..."'

He put an arm around her waist and led her down a long hallway towards an enormous drawing-room where a large group of people, all dressed in formal clothes, were milling about. There was a steady buzz of conversation, the clink of glasses, the sound of music playing in the background.

Before she stepped inside, Regan had one more attack of nerves, but when she saw that all the women were dressed as formally as she was, and several of the younger ones in gowns far more revealing than hers, her courage returned. Jack's reassuring arm around her also helped.

She scanned the room quickly, looking for Nick, but if he was there she could see no sign of him.

'Let's get you a drink,' Jack was saying as they made their way towards a long bar set up at the far end of the room. 'Then I'll introduce you around.'

She had already spotted several of the lawyers she'd been working with recently, so at least she'd have someone to talk to. As it turned out, she needn't have worried, since Jack Lombardi stuck to her like glue throughout most of the evening, plying her with wine, before, during and after supper.

It was when they were on their way to the buffet table in the dining room that she finally saw Nick. He hadn't yet sat down to eat, and was standing by the doors to the terrace in a small group, a drink in his hand. He looked devastating in his dinner-jacket. His dark hair and tanned skin seemed to glow against the brilliant white of his stiff collar and shirt.

A slim, blonde woman in an elegant long black dress was standing close beside him, her arm linked in his, looking up at him adoringly and hanging on his every word. Regan thought about the stewardess on the plane. Obviously, his taste ran to blondes. This one looked as though she were glued to him.

Then she felt Jack tighten his hold around her waist. 'Come on,' he said. 'Let's go find something to eat. Ma has a magician of a caterer.'

That possessive arm around her waist made her uncomfortable, but every time she tried to edge away from him he only pulled her closer.

'I really should go over and speak to my boss,' she murmured.

'That's your boss?' he enquired. 'Nick Wainwright?'

His tone was so incredulous that Regan turned to him and gave him a searching look. 'Yes. You sound surprised.'

He made an offhand gesture. 'Well, I was just putting two and two together. I mean, Nick comes from Seattle, and if he's your boss, that means you're travelling with him...' His voice trailed off apologetically.

'If you're thinking what I think you're thinking, you can forget it,' she said firmly. 'That's not the way we operate in Seattle, at least not in our firm.'

His hand moved slowly up from her waist to her bare back. 'Well, that's a relief,' he said with a warm smile. 'You didn't seem like his usual type. Come on, forget the job for one night. This is a party, remember? You can check in with the boss later.'

She turned to give Nick one last dubious look, and just at that moment, he looked up. When he saw her, his eyes widened slightly, then narrowed, his features darkening in a frown.

For some reason, that look made Regan feel guilty, as though she had no right to be there. Yet he was the one who had virtually commanded her to attend in the first place. She turned back to Jack and smiled up at him.

'All right,' she said. 'Let's go eat.'

After they had filled their plates, they wandered back through the crowded drawing-room. 'It's still a pleasant evening,' Jack said, leading the way towards one of the small tables set up out on the paved terrace. 'Let's eat outside while it's still light.'

Regan's nervousness had pretty well dissipated by now, thanks to the wine she'd been drinking and the assiduous attentions of Jack Lombardi. She wasn't used to that kind of interest from men. He treated her as though she was a desirable woman, not a lackey or an inferior man, as her fellow male lawyers were likely to do, and it was an extremely pleasant sensation.

'So, how long are you going to be in town?' Jack asked over dinner. 'I'd like to see you again, show you the sights of our fair city. How about this weekend?'

'We're leaving on Friday, I'm sorry,' she said.

'But you'll be back. My father tells me that the trial is coming up in a few weeks. Those things can take weeks. Surely you'll have some free time.' He reached across the table and covered her hand with his. 'I really like you, Regan,' he said in a low intimate tone. 'I hope we can be friends.'

Regan knew quite well what he meant by that, but she was having too good a time to much care at this point. Although Jack was obviously the spoiled, idle son of a wealthy family, used to getting his own way, here was a handsome man interested in something besides her mind. And he *was* quite handsome, pretty even, with almost feminine features.

She gave him a dazzling smile and was about to say something to encourage him, when all of a sudden the wine she had drunk during the evening hit her. A wave of dizziness passed over her, and her stomach began to churn. She knew she'd better get up and walk around immediately before it was too late.

She rose unsteadily to her feet. 'Excuse me a minute, Jack. I'll be right back.'

'Are you all right?' he asked, half rising out of his chair.

'I'm fine. The powder-room, you know.'

She tottered off, concentrating on every step, and finally found a small bathroom at the far end of a long hall. It was unoccupied, thankfully, and she slipped inside and locked the door behind her.

At the sink she bathed her face in cold water, then sat down and put her head down between her legs. After a few minutes, it began to clear. She got up and splashed more cold water on her face and wrists, then went back out into the hall to look for a telephone so she could call a cab. She'd put in her appearance, now it was time to leave before she disgraced herself.

She had only taken a few steps, however, when she suddenly came face to face with Nick Wainwright. He was just standing there, his arms folded over his chest, and if looks could kill she would have dropped dead on the spot.

'Hi,' she said weakly.

'I hope you're proud of yourself,' he said in a scathing tone. His stony eyes swept her up and down. 'Is this what you call professional behaviour? You look like someone who just came in off the streets.'

Regan quailed in her new high-heeled sandals. Her first instinct was to apologise, defend herself, try to wriggle out of the tight spot she was in. But the drink had given her a kind of Dutch courage, a feeling of daring that was new to her, but intensely exhilarating. He was furious, that was clear, but at least he'd noticed her as something besides a flunkey to carry his bags and stamp his documents and get his coffee.

She sauntered slowly towards him, wiggling her hips just a little, until she was directly in front of him, almost touching him. To her in her high heels he didn't seem quite so tall or nearly so forbidding. She looked up at him with a smile, her head cocked to one side, and batted her eyes.

'Why, Nick,' she purred innocently. 'Weren't you the one who advised me that if I had it I should flaunt it?'

For one second she was certain he was going to strike her. His face grew livid, his eyes were narrowed into slits. Her face was so close to his that she could see the pulse pounding along his jawline. Then, from behind her came a voice calling her name. It was Jack.

'Regan? Are you OK?'

She turned around. 'Yes, Jack, I'm fine. I was looking for a telephone to call a cab. It's getting late, and we have a long day ahead of us tomorrow.'

'I'll drive you home if you really have to go,' he replied, coming towards her.

'Oh, that would be lovely,' she gushed, primarily for Nick's benefit.

Giving Nick one last dazzling smile and flutter of eyelashes, she put her arm through Jack's and walked off with him down the hall, leaving Nick standing there, his fists clenched at his sides, still seething with outrage and fury for all she knew.

In the middle of the night, Regan woke up with a pounding headache. It was dark out, but she had no idea what time it was. Groaning aloud, she reached out blindly to switch on the lamp, then turned carefully on her side to look for her watch on the bedside table. At even that slight cautious movement, it felt as though fresh nails were being driven into her skull.

She eased her head back on the pillow with another piteous moan. What difference did it make what time it was? She just wished she were dead. What had possessed her to consume all that wine when ordinarily she didn't drink at all?

Her one thought now was to get up and find something for her headache. After a few minutes, she tried opening her eyes again in gradual stages, and as the room came into focus she raised herself up again and shook her head gently in an effort to clear it. She had some aspirin in her handbag. All she had to do was find it.

She eased herself out of bed and groped around on every available surface, but after several moments of fruitless searching she gave it up. She'd probably dropped it off somewhere in the living-room on her way to bed.

She went over to the bedroom door, opened it, and stepped out into the hall. There was a dim light still burning in the living-room, and she made her way towards it, step by agonising step.

When she reached it, she peered cautiously inside and to her horror saw that Nick was there. He was standing at the table, half turned away from her, looking down at the documents stacked on top. Her first impulse was to turn and scurry back to her bedroom, but she was suddenly paralysed, unable to move a muscle, and could only stand and stare.

He was bare-chested, wearing only the black trousers of his formal suit, and Regan couldn't tear her eyes away from the sight of all that tanned, muscular, very masculine flesh. His dark hair was rumpled and falling over his forehead. She'd only ever seen him before immaculate and fully dressed, and this unexpected apparition was setting up some strange stirring sensations deep inside her.

Her headache was forgotten. She didn't even feel it. She stood there staring at him for several long seconds before it finally occurred to her that if she didn't get out of there in a hurry he'd see her, too. But it was too late. He'd already turned around, his eyes flicking over her.

It was then she realised that all she had on was a thin nightgown, but it was too late for that, too. She'd just have to face it out.

She darted a quick glance around the room and finally spotted her handbag, still sitting on the table where she'd left it. Hugging her arms around her to cover the low bodice of her nightgown, she raised her chin and made directly for the table with as much dignity as she could muster in the circumstances, avoiding the eyes that she knew were fastened upon her every step of the way.

'I just wanted to get some aspirin out of my bag,' she mumbled as she reached past him.

'What's the matter?' he drawled nastily. 'Got a headache?'

She was so close to him now that she could hear his quick breath in the dead silence of the dim room, almost feel the warmth of his body. Darting him a swift sideways glance, she grabbed hold of her bag.

'I'm not surprised,' he went on in a smug voice. 'You certainly seemed to be enjoying yourself at the party tonight. Now you're paying for it.'

The shock of seeing him there half-naked had miraculously cured the pounding in her head, but enough lingering effects of the wine still remained to give her courage. She whirled around to face him.

'What's wrong with you, anyway?' she demanded. 'I don't understand what you've got to complain about. *You* told me to go to the party, and I went. *You* told me to get out of my "uniform", and I did that, too.'

He bent down and stuck his face close to hers. 'I didn't tell you to make a spectacle of yourself!' he ground out accusingly. 'Dressing like a streetwalker, getting drunk.'

'I was not drunk!' she shouted.

'And hanging all over Jack Lombardi,' he droned inexorably on. 'A shallow playboy with a reputation for——'

'Hah!' she exclaimed, really angry now. 'You're one to talk about reputations!'

He raised one heavy eyebrow, then nodded and smiled thinly with grim satisfaction. 'Ah,' he said. 'So that's it. You're just mad because I haven't made a move on you myself.'

Virtually beside herself with fury by now, she raised an arm and swung her bag at his face with all her might. But, before it could connect, one long arm shot up, grabbed hold of her wrist and forced it back.

They stood there, glaring at each other, their eyes locked together, for what seemed like an eternity.

'You're hurting me,' she said at last.

'Good!' he snapped. 'I should put you over my knee and spank you.'

Then, suddenly, his eyes dropped lower and fastened on her heaving breast. The hand on her wrist loosened its iron grip, but still he didn't release her. She could smell the liquor on his breath, and realised that he'd had more than enough to drink himself.

He raised his eyes again, and this time the anger in them was gone. In its place was a bright gleam that was vaguely familiar to her. She'd seen it there once or twice before, but it had always disappeared before she'd recognised it. Now she knew. It was naked desire, pure and simple.

There was a choking sensation in her throat, and she drew in a sharp gasping breath. She couldn't tear her eyes away from that compelling silvery gaze. His fingers seemed to be burning a hole in her skin where he held her, and she began to shiver uncontrollably.

The next thing she knew, his arms had come around her, and he was pressing her up against his broad chest. Without thinking, she leaned into him and raised her hands up to the back of his neck. As her fingers raked through his dark smooth hair, she suddenly realised how much she had been longing to do this, ever since the first day she met him.

His mouth was on hers now, seeking, his tongue thrusting past her lips. Eagerly, she returned his kiss, and when she felt his hand move around to fasten on her breast she made a little noise deep in her throat at the delicious sensations his touch aroused in her.

His lower body was grinding against hers now, and she could feel his hard arousal. His hands were everywhere, stroking her bare back, slipping inside the low-cut bodice of her nightgown to clutch feverishly at her breasts. She felt as though she were drowning, but prayed it would never end.

Suddenly, she felt his body grow taut. He tore his mouth away from hers, and clamped his hands on her shoulders, pushing her away from him. He was still breathing hard, but the look of desire in his eyes was gone, and what she saw now was a kind of horrified shock.

He dropped his hands from her shoulders, and turned from her. She watched him as he struggled for control, wondering what had happened to make him change so suddenly. After a few moments, he turned back to her, seemingly quite composed once again.

'We have a long day ahead of us tomorrow, McIntyre,' he said in the old brusque tone. 'You've got your aspirin. I suggest you take some. I'm going to bed.'

He turned then, and walked away from her, leaving Regan standing there gazing after him in utter bewilderment. When he was gone, she picked her bag up off the floor where she had dropped it, and went slowly down the hall to her bedroom.

CHAPTER FIVE

THE next day it was as though nothing out of the ordinary had ever happened between them. They followed their usual morning routine, and their conversations consisted entirely of the business at hand. Not by a word or a look or a gesture did Nick refer to that midnight encounter, not then, nor for the remainder of their stay.

In time Regan came to believe that she'd dreamt the whole thing. She'd had too much to drink, she'd awakened in the middle of the night, still groggy, and must have had a hallucination. She didn't entirely believe this version, but Nick kept her too busy to dwell on it.

Jack Lombardi called her twice in the next few days, but she always managed to put him off, pleading the pressure of work. It wasn't really a lie. Nick worked her hard from early morning until late at night, when she would fall into bed exhausted.

By Friday, there only remained a few minor details to settle, and the meeting broke up at noon. The flight back to Seattle was scheduled for six o'clock, which gave Regan just time enough to pack and get all those documents in their proper cartons ready for shipment back to Seattle. Just one more week and the trial would start. Nick hadn't said anything about wanting her with him for it, but she still had hopes. He hadn't complained once about her work.

That afternoon, as she folded the new silk dress carefully in tissue paper, it reminded her again of the night of the party. It was the first real opportunity she'd had to think about it. Had it happened after all? Or had it been only a dream?

It might as well have been, since the one certainty in her mind was that if she and Nick were to continue working together there could be no question of personal involvement. Still, even if it had been only a dream, it was a very pleasant one to remember.

Nick was waiting for her in the living-room when she'd finished packing, and she was surprised to see that instead of wearing a business suit for travelling he had on his dinner-jacket again.

'Are you all ready to go?' he asked.

'Yes,' she replied, puzzled. 'How about you?'

'Oh, I'm not leaving tonight,' he said offhandedly. Then he grinned. 'I have a date.'

'But what about the documents? We still have to pack up the files.'

'Oh, you can do that,' he said airily.

Then she saw red. 'And what if *I* happen to have a date?' she demanded.

'Do you?'

'Well, no, but Jack has called several times——'

'Then get to work, McIntyre,' he broke in abruptly.

My master's voice, she thought, as he started for his room. When he was gone, she frowned angrily down at the documents. Nick's high-handed attitude infuriated her, but what else could she do but obey?

Heaving a deep sigh of self-pity at the injustice of it all, she started picking up folders and stacking them into cartons, but, before long, as her anger grew, she found herself slamming them around noisily and throwing them inside any old way.

Nick came back in a few minutes, his hands in his trouser pockets, jingling change and keys and whistling under his breath. On his way past the table to the door he glanced sharply at her.

'Hey, be a little more careful with that stuff,' he said. 'What are you trying to do, kill it?'

By now she was more than ready to kill *him*, and she whirled around to face him. 'Listen,' she said. 'It's not fair. You've treated me like your slave ever since the first day I came to work for you, just because you resent the fact that I'm a woman who can do a man's job, and I'm fed up.'

He looked down his nose at her. 'I've told you before, McIntyre. We all have to go through a certain amount of slave labour in the beginning. I'm not going to make an exception just because you're a woman. If you want special treatment, you'd better look for it somewhere else, because you won't get it from me.'

Regan bit her lip and fought down her anger. He was right. Nothing would be gained by antagonising him any more than she already had just for the sake of a personal grudge. She knew when she was beaten. She was skating on thin ice as it was.

'Yes, sir,' she muttered through her teeth.

She turned back to the hateful files and started straightening out the mess she'd made. Nick seemed to hesitate for a second, and she wondered what he was going to ask her to do this time. Pack for him, perhaps. Well, whatever it was, she'd do it if it killed her and keep her mouth shut about it.

Then she heard his footsteps as he walked away from her, heard him open the door and close it again behind him. When she was sure he was gone, she looked up and glared at the door, suppressed the urge to throw the file in her hand against it, and once again got back to work.

On the flight back to Seattle early that evening, it seemed strange to Regan not to have Nick sitting beside her. Even though she was still simmering at the shabby way he'd treated her, they'd been together so constantly during the past five days that his absence left a real void. At least, she consoled herself, she wouldn't have to watch him ogling the stewardess.

Once the plane was safely airborne, she lay her head back and closed her eyes, but she found she was still too keyed up from that last-minute rush to sleep. Nick had kept her so busy that this was the first real chance she'd had to try to put the events of the past week in some kind of perspective.

All in all, she was satisfied that she'd done a good job for him. Even though she'd flared up at him a few times when his critical comments became personal, for the most part she'd followed him around and done his bidding like a faithful dog. She was grateful now that she'd held her tongue this afternoon when he'd announced the news that she would have to do all the packing herself because he had a date.

She wondered who it was. The blonde stewardess from the trip down last Sunday? The elegant blonde who'd been hanging all over him at the party? Always blondes, she thought in disgust as she unconsciously ran a hand over her own light-brown hair.

With the drone of the engine buzzing in her ears, her mind wandered idly back to that night of the party and the eerie encounter with Nick in the middle of the night. At the time she had convinced herself it had been a dream, but now, with the pressure of business off and the leisure to consider it more thoroughly, she wasn't so sure.

Even if it had really happened, no doubt it was because they'd both had too much to drink earlier. Not only that, but it was over practically before it started. Yet, as she finally drifted off into a fitful sleep, it seemed to her that she could still feel that bare chest pressed against her, his arms holding her, the taste of his seeking mouth, his hand on her breast.

The next thing she knew, they were landing at the Seattle airport. After collecting her bag, she went out in front to look for a cab. There was no point in calling Don to come and get her, as he'd offered. The Friday night traffic would be horrendous, and Don, who was even more overworked than she was, needed all the rest he could get. She'd just put the taxi fare on her expense account, and Nick could lump it if he didn't like it. She'd earned it.

It was a lovely summer evening, the sun still shining at after seven o'clock, and, as the cab sped north on the motorway towards the city, Regan gazed out of the window at the familiar landmarks, the mountains to the east and west, the blue waters of Puget Sound and Lake Union, thinking how glad she was to be home. Seattle had never looked so good to her.

Her apartment was hot and stuffy, and as soon as she was inside she ran around opening windows. Her first goal was a warm shower. She could save the unpacking for later. Tomorrow was Saturday. She'd have the whole weekend to go grocery shopping and do her laundry.

She had finished her shower, dried off and was just wrapping a towel around her wet head, when there came a loud knocking at her front door. Quickly, she pulled on clean underwear, a pair of jeans and a cotton shirt and ran barefoot to answer it.

'Yes,' she called. 'Who is it?'

'Regan?' came Don's worried voice. 'Is that you? Are you home?'

She opened the door. 'Come on in, Don.'

'I heard noises down here and thought I'd better investigate.' He stepped inside, closing the door after him. 'You were supposed to call me when you got in.'

'Oh, I didn't want to bother you.' They were into the living-room. 'Sit down for a minute if you have time.'

'Have you eaten?'

'No,' she said in surprise. 'I haven't, as a matter of fact.' She laughed. 'I was so glad to be home I forgot all about food.'

'How about sharing a pizza?'

'OK.' She pointed at the telephone in the hall. 'Why don't you call and have one delivered? I still have a few things to do.'

While Don made the call, Regan went back into the bathroom and picked up after herself. Her hair was not quite dry, so she used the drier on it for a few minutes, then brushed it back behind her ears, put on a dash of pale coral lip gloss, slipped into a pair of moccasins and went back to the living-room.

'Well,' Don said, as she sat down opposite him on the couch. 'How was the trip?'

She made a face. 'Harrowing. That boss of mine is a real slave driver.'

'In what way?'

'Oh, you name it. It's "Go do this, McIntyre,"' she mimicked Nick's deep voice. '"Make five hundred copies, get me a cup of coffee, pack those boxes."' She made a wry face. 'I expected him to put me to work shining his shoes or pressing his suits by the time we were through.'

Don was laughing by now. 'Tell me about it!' he said with feeling. 'I've got a cardiologist at the hospital who must have learned his tricks in the same school.'

When the boy came with their pizza, Don paid him, then they went into the kitchen and sat down at the small table by the window. Don sliced the pizza while Regan got two bottles of beer out of the refrigerator, and they sat down to eat.

'Have you ever thought of asking for another assignment?' Don asked between bites. 'I mean, if your boss is that hard to please, maybe you should consider it. They can't all be that bad.'

Regan slowly set down her glass and looked at him. 'Why, no,' she said soberly. 'That never entered my mind.' She shrugged. 'Oh, granted, he's impossible, but working for him gives me the chance to learn from one of the best legal minds in the city. How about you and your problem doctor? Would you leave him?'

Don laughed. 'Interns don't leave doctors. Doctors fire interns.' Then his expression grew serious. 'And to answer your question, no, I wouldn't dream of it. Like your boss, he's terrible to deal with, but there's not another doctor around who could teach me as much about cardiology as he can.'

'Well, then, you should be able to understand the way I feel about Nick Wainwright.' She eyed the carton on the table. 'I'll toss you for the last slice.'

*   *   *

Regan virtually slept the weekend away. She hadn't realised just how exhausted she was from the gruelling sessions in San Francisco until she was back in her own bed. Then she could hardly bear to get out of it, except to do the most essential shopping and a little laundry on Saturday between naps.

The weather remained fine, and by late Sunday afternoon she was beginning to feel rested at last. She took a long walk around Green Lake, had a light supper at her place, then spent the rest of the evening getting ready for work the next day. Nick should be back, and she was amazed at how much she looked forward to the prospect of seeing him again.

She arrived at the office bright and early Monday morning and headed directly towards her own small office. It was good to be back, and as she walked by the library the other young lawyers labouring inside called to her, welcoming her back warmly, as though they really were glad to see her, making her feel as though she really belonged now.

She went directly to Nick's office, assuming he would already be there. It was past nine o'clock, and she hoped he wouldn't give her a dressing down for being late. When she glanced inside, there was no sign of him, but Sheila was there sitting at his desk and going through a stack of mail. She looked up when she saw Regan.

'Welcome back,' she said. 'How was the trip?'

'I think it went OK,' Regan replied. 'At least we covered most of the pre-trial work and pretty much agreed about procedure. Where's Nick?'

'Oh, he's still in San Francisco.'

Regan stared at her. 'I thought he was coming back over the weekend.'

'No, he called me at home late Friday night. The judge who will be hearing the case had a last-minute cancellation in his docket, so we go to trial today instead of next week.'

'I see.' She hesitated. 'I guess he didn't say anything about my going back down there, or if he needed me to do anything for him here?'

Sheila looked up from the mail. 'I don't know. He didn't say.' She smiled. 'If I know Nick, you'll hear from him the minute he does want something.'

'Yes. Of course,' Regan said. 'You're right.'

She left Nick's office and started walking slowly to her own room next door, fighting the dull ache in her heart, the tears of disappointment that stung behind her eyes.

She should have known better than to get her hopes up in the first place. He'd made it clear that the assignment was only for one week of pre-trial work, and the most menial aspects of it at that. She hadn't actually practised any law at all, unless you could count stamping documents, taking notes, packing boxes of files and putting up with his nasty disposition.

Besides, it was unreasonable to expect to be wafted into the rarefied atmosphere of an actual trial at the very beginning of her career, and, if she expected to compete with the big boys, she'd have to start by taking these little blows to her ego in her stride.

When she reached her office, the telephone on her desk was ringing. That could be him now. She ran over to the desk, dropped her handbag on top and snatched up the receiver.

'Regan McIntyre,' she said.

'Welcome back,' came Jim Courtney's voice. 'How did it go down there?'

'Quite well, I think.'

'Good.' He paused for a moment. 'Listen, Regan, if you have a minute could you come up to my office? There's something I need to discuss with you.'

'Yes, of course,' she said. 'Right away.'

After she hung up she stood there for a long time, her hand still on the telephone, wondering what it could be he wanted to talk to her about. Probably more office trivia, she supposed, thinking of those endless personnel forms she'd already filled out.

She made her way up the inside staircase to the floor above, still disappointed that the telephone call had not been from Nick, but determined not to let it show.

Jim Courtney was in his large corner office, absorbed in a file spread out on top of his desk. The bright morning sunshine was streaming in through the windows behind him, and the snow-capped mountains gleamed in the background beyond the harbour.

When Regan rapped lightly on the door, he looked up and smiled at her. 'Come in, Regan. Have a seat.'

She took the chair across from him and watched him as he got up to adjust the blinds so that the sun wouldn't shine directly in her eyes. He sat down again, leaned back in his swivel chair and gave her a long close look.

'I wanted to talk to you about your new assignment,' he said without any preamble.

Regan goggled at him. 'What new assignment?'

'Now that your job on the pharmaceutical case is finished, you'll be working with me on a merger of two small local banks.' He smiled. 'Not as exciting as antitrust work, but it'll be good experience for you, and I really need some help.'

Regan swallowed the lump in her throat. 'I see.'

Jim Courtney laughed. 'You don't sound as though you're exactly thrilled at the news.'

She forced out a weak smile. 'Sorry. I guess it just took me a little by surprise. I mean, I really do like antitrust work, and I was hoping...' Her voice trailed off.

'Yes, I know. But you do understand that we rotate all our young lawyers from one branch of the law to another from time to time. It's standard practice. I have the bank merger file right here, and I'd like you to take it with you. Study it carefully until you familiarise yourself with what's been done so far, then write me a memo setting out——'

'Mr Courtney,' she interrupted. She gazed at him earnestly. 'I don't mean to step out of line, but I have to know. Did Nick request that I be taken off the case?'

He gazed at her for some moments, his light blue eyes kindly behind the glasses, obviously debating within himself. Finally, he heaved a sigh and levered himself out of his chair. He came around to the front of the desk, leaned back against it, and crossed his arms in front of him.

'No,' he said at last. 'He didn't.'

She searched his face. 'But he agreed to it.'

'Yes.'

Regan's heart sank. She knew he could have kept her on if he'd wanted to. She rose slowly to her feet and raised her chin. 'Did he complain about my work?'

'No, he didn't,' he said slowly. 'As a matter of fact, he went to great lengths to praise you, said you were a great help.'

'Then it's because I'm a woman, isn't it?' Before he could reply, she rushed on. 'I thought that was all straightened out before I came, that he'd changed his mind about that. Or that you had changed it for him.'

'Regan,' he said patiently, 'Nick was in total agreement that we should hire you. We're not firing you, after all. There's no question of that. We're only reassigning you. It's our policy, standard procedure. It's no reflection on you whatsoever. As I told you, Nick himself has the highest regard for your abilities.'

'Maybe if I talked to him——' she began.

He held up a hand to stop her. 'Listen to me, Regan,' he said in a sterner tone. 'Nick Wainwright is our best antitrust lawyer. His case is going to trial a week sooner than he expected. He'll be under terrific pressure, not only from the defendants, but from his own fellow plaintiffs. I'm the managing partner, and this was my decision. For whatever reason, Nick did agree, but now it's no longer his concern and I don't want him worried over it. In any case, he's too fine a professional to allow his personal feelings about working with a woman to interfere with a case, but, even if he did believe he couldn't work up to his maximum efficiency because of a woman's presence, then that would be it, as far as I'm concerned.'

Regan knew when she was beaten. Better to bow out now with as good grace as she could muster than make an issue of it. He didn't want her badly enough to insist on keeping her, and that was final. At least he hadn't complained about her work.

'I'm sorry,' she said at last. 'I guess I'm just a little disappointed. I thought things went so well in San Francisco.'

'I'm sure they did.' He handed her the file and led her to the door. 'Now for the good news,' he said, going into the room next to his. 'This will be your new office. Quite an improvement, don't you agree? You can move up here right away.'

Regan glanced around. It was small, but a paradise compared with the cramped cubbyhole she'd been using. There was a window with a pleasant view of the harbour, a good-looking bookcase, and a brand new filing cabinet, without Nick's voluminous documents cluttering the top of it.

She turned to Jim Courtney. 'It's wonderful,' she said. 'Thank you. And I know I'll enjoy working with you.'

She left him then and walked slowly back down to her old room to collect her belongings. She'd managed to put on a brave front for Jim Courtney, but her heart was still heavy. In spite of Nick Wainwright's difficult temperament, she had really hoped to continue working with him. The pleasant and more spacious new office was small consolation for the loss of that.

By Friday of that week, Regan was deep into the arcane mysteries of bank mergers, and almost blind from poring over the fine print in the endless agreements, contracts, warranties and deeds she had to plod through every day. It was the excitement of trial work that really interested her, and by now she was half bored out of her mind.

Jim Courtney was a dream to work for compared with Nick. Not only was he more considerate of her feelings, but he took the time to explain exactly what he wanted from her when he gave her a job to do and treated her as though she were an actual human being instead of his personal slave. He even got his own coffee. And it was pleasant to be able to look out of the window at a gorgeous view instead of staring at a wall filled with broken-down filing cabinets.

But all the zest seemed to have gone out of her job. She no longer looked forward to going to work each morning the way she had when she was working with Nick. She kept telling herself she'd get used to it in time, but the time was passing mighty slowly.

She'd even begun to take regular breaks twice a day, something she had rarely done under Nick's absolute dictatorship. The coffee-room was located on the floor below her new office, and as she went down the stairs that afternoon she had to admit that one of the attractions of those breaks was that she had to pass by her old office—and Nick's—on her way.

She hadn't seen him or even heard anything about him or how his trial was going since she got back. Her old office appeared to be unoccupied, and Nick's was still empty, the growing stacks of mail arranged neatly on his desk.

She passed on to the small room on the other side, where Sheila was sitting at her desk, typing busily. Regan stood there for a moment in the doorway watching her until the blonde secretary finally raised her eyes and smiled at her.

'Hello, Regan,' she said. 'How go the deeds and contracts?'

Mills & Boon

Discover
FREE BOOKS
— AND —
FREE GIFTS
From Mills & Boon

As a special introduction to
Mills & Boon Romances we will send you:

FOUR FREE Mills & Boon Romances plus a **FREE TEDDY** and **MYSTERY GIFT** when you return this card.

But first - just for fun - see if you can find and circle four hidden words in the puzzle.

R	D	A	V	R	Y	B	X	N	M
B	O	O	K	N	C	A	S	P	Y
Z	G	M	N	B	U	L	T	R	S
R	T	N	A	N	E	F	T	A	T
D	H	I	A	N	V	K	D	M	E
N	W	L	K	H	C	O	W	S	R
O	C	O	M	U	T	E	D	D	Y
I	L	V	F	L	P	B	I	T	E
F	E	E	J	S	G	I	F	T	P
S	P	N	S	E	T	I	N	R	E

The hidden words are:

MYSTERY
ROMANCE
TEDDY
GIFT

Now turn over to claim your
FREE BOOKS AND GIFTS

Free Books Certificate

Yes! Please send me four specially selected Mills & Boon Romances, together with my FREE Teddy and Mystery Gift. I would also like you to reserve a special Reader Service Subscription for me. Which means that I can go on to enjoy six brand new Romances sent to me each month for just £8.70, postage and packing FREE. If I decide not to subscribe I shall write to you within 10 days. Any FREE books and gifts will remain mine to keep. I understand that I am under no obligation whatsoever - I can cancel or suspend my subscription at any time simply by writing to you. I am over 18 years of age.

4A1R

Mrs/Miss/Mr _____

Address _____

_____

_____

_____ Postcode _____

Signature _____

FREE TEDDY

MYSTERY GIFT

Reader Service
FREEPOST
P.O. Box 236
Croydon
Surrey CR9 9EL

The right is reserved to refuse an application and change the terms of this offer. Offer expires 31st Dec 1991. You may be mailed with offers from Mills & Boon and other reputable companies as a result of this application. If you would prefer not to share in this opportunity, please tick box ☐

Readers in Southern Africa write to: Independent Book Services Pty. Postbag X3010 Randburg 2125. South Africa.   * Overseas and Eire send for details.

Regan made a face. 'Don't ask.' She paused a moment, then said casually, 'Any news from the wars in San Francisco?'

'Not a word. I haven't heard from the boss all week. There's probably nothing to report just yet. The preliminaries of a trial are pretty much boring routine as a rule.'

'Yes, I suppose so,' Regan said, and with a little wave went on by.

Not half so boring as bank mergers, she thought bitterly as she went inside the coffee-room. It was always crowded at this hour of the afternoon, when the whole office seemed to gather there. The two other women lawyers, Margaret and Laura, were sitting alone at a table, however, and after Regan poured herself a cup of coffee she went over to join them.

'Well, Regan,' Laura said after she'd sat down. 'How was San Francisco?'

'Not bad. Hectic.'

'I hear you're off the pharmaceutical case and working for Jim Courtney now,' Margaret said. 'How come? Did you have your fill of Nick Wainwright?'

'Something like that,' Regan murmured non-committally.

Laura leaned towards her. 'I bet I know what happened,' she said in a low confidential tone. 'He made a move on you, didn't he?'

'Of course not,' Regan replied stoutly. 'You know his rule about that.'

Laura laughed. 'Well, one can still dream. Rules are meant to be broken, you know. I wouldn't mind a shot at him myself. At least he's not married.'

She then launched into a piteous tale of how her married lover had decided to stay with his wife and family after all. The moment she drew breath, Margaret chimed in with her own recitation of grievances about the hardships of trying to balance career and family.

Although Regan was glad not to be the focus of their attention any longer, she only half listened to their familiar complaints, all of which she had heard so many times before that she knew them by heart.

In any event, she certainly found no joy in their company, and after gulping her coffee down hastily she got up and left them to their misery. As she walked slowly back upstairs to face her tedious merger again, a heavy, lethargic depression descended on her—about her job, her relationships, her whole life.

When Regan got home that evening, she found Don sitting on the floor in front of her apartment, slouched back against the door. He was frowning down at a thick textbook, but when he saw her his face lit up and he jumped to his feet.

'I've been waiting for you,' he said, grinning broadly.

'So I see,' she replied, smiling at him in spite of her black mood. She stuck her key in the lock, and he followed her inside.

'I wanted to catch you before you collapsed,' he went on. 'I know what Friday nights are like.'

'Well, here I am. What can I do for you?'

'Miracle of miracles, I have the evening off, and thought I'd try to talk you into going out for a hamburger with me.'

'Oh, Don, I'm dead beat. I've just put in the most boring week of my life.'

'Well, you have to eat. And once you sit down you know darned well you won't get up until Sunday. We can hoof it around the corner to McDonald's and be back in an hour. Come on. It'll do you good.'

Regan looked at him. He was probably right. Besides that, there was something about him that cheered her up. Just the sight of him with his silly lopsided grin, his tattered jeans and sloppy sweatshirt, his good humour, made her forget her own sour mood.

'All right,' she said at last. 'But we go Dutch or we don't go at all. Understood?'

He lifted his skinny shoulders and spread his arms wide. 'I won't argue with that. I'm only a struggling intern, and you know what kind of poverty-level salary they make. Tell you what, when I'm a rich doctor I'll take you out in style to the most expensive restaurant in town.'

Regan nodded. 'You've got yourself a deal. Thanks, Don. I feel better already.'

He wiggled his shaggy, sandy eyebrows and made a funny face at her. Then, putting on a heavily accented voice, he said, 'What are friends for?'

That broke Regan up, and while she was still laughing at him, all of a sudden his comical look slowly vanished, and his expression grew serious. He put his hands lightly on her shoulders and gave her a direct look.

'I mean it, too,' he said soberly. 'About the expensive restaurant. I know I'm not in any position right now to make any commitments, but I really like you, Regan, and I hope in time we can be more than friends. Much more.'

Regan stared at him. With her heels on, they were almost exactly the same height, and as their eyes met, a deep flush washed over his face. It had never occurred to her that Don might be interested in her that way, and it was hard for her to think of him romantically at all. He was a dear, good friend, but that was all.

'Well,' she said lightly, moving slightly away from him. 'We'll talk about that when you're a rich doctor.'

He dropped his hands to his sides and gave her a crooked, knowing smile, as though to say he knew exactly what she was thinking but didn't intend to give up that easily.

After dinner, they went for a short walk, and it was dark by the time Don left her at her door. When she stepped inside her apartment, the telephone was ringing. She went into the hall and picked up the receiver.

'Hello,' she said.

'Regan?'

It was a man's voice, but she couldn't quite place it. 'Yes, this is she.'

'This is Nick. Nick Wainwright.'

She stared down at the receiver in her hand. Nick? But it couldn't be. He never called her Regan.

'Regan,' came the voice again. 'Are you there?'

'Yes,' she replied slowly. 'I'm here. But I thought you were still in San Francisco.'

'I was, but, since it's the long Fourth of July weekend anyway, our judge very kindly gave us a week's recess.'

'I see,' she said. But why was he calling her? Maybe he wanted her back on the case. She wanted that more than anything, but it wouldn't do to appear too eager, so she only waited.

'I'm calling to see if you're free for dinner tomorrow night.'

'Why?' It was all she could think of to say.

He gave a short, dry bark of a laugh. 'Why? Because I want you to have it with me.'

CHAPTER SIX

REGAN sank slowly down on the chair beside the telephone table. She could hardly believe her ears. It was the last thing in the world she would ever have expected. She must have misunderstood Nick. It wouldn't do to jump to conclusions. She still had her job to consider. He just might want her back on the case.

'I'm not sure I understand,' she said in a guarded tone.

'It's simple enough, isn't it?' he enquired with a touch of impatience. 'I'm asking you to have dinner with me tomorrow night.'

'What for?'

He laughed. 'What for? What do men usually call and invite women out for?'

A slow anger began to rise up from deep within her, and as it grew, she threw caution—and probably her job—to the winds.

'You've got a nerve,' she spluttered when she was able to speak. 'After what you did to me, what makes you think I'd want to go out anywhere on earth with you?'

'What did I ever do to you?' he asked innocently.

The undertone of amusement in his voice only fed the flames. 'You agreed to take me off the pharmaceutical case, that's what you did to me!' She was almost shouting by now.

102

'Well, I had to, didn't I?' he commented equably. 'How else could I ask you out?'

She was utterly speechless as this revelation penetrated the red haze of her anger. Suddenly there flashed into her mind a vision of that midnight encounter in San Francisco. Whatever had made her think it was a dream? What was more, it obviously had lingered in his memory too, even had the same effect on him that it had on her.

'Listen, Regan,' he went on in a more placating tone. 'Your work was fine. I made that clear to Jim Courtney. You'll be a damn good lawyer one of these days. But at the moment I have something else in mind.'

Now that he'd clarified his motive in calling her and asking her out, she began to calm down. He actually seemed to be interested in her as a woman! This put him in an entirely new light. The question was, should she accept? More to the point, did she *want* to accept?

Her mind raced. What would be the harm? As far as her job was concerned, no one in the office needed to know about it. Not only was he famous for keeping his private life separate from his work, their offices were even on different floors. Besides, he'd be away at his trial for weeks, possibly months.

She was strongly tempted. She wanted to go. The only thing stopping her was that she didn't want to be just another notch on his belt. But far outweighing that concern was her growing sense of the sheer boredom of her life. Her job seemed to have reached a dead end, at least for the time being. There were no other promising men in sight. She was intrigued by this sudden unexpected move of his. And she was definitely attracted to him.

Finally, she made up her mind. Taking a deep breath, she said, 'All right, Nick. I'll go out to dinner with you tomorrow night.'

'Good,' he replied promptly. 'I'll pick you up at seven o'clock.'

After they'd hung up, Regan sat there motionless for some time, grinning foolishly, her heart pounding wildly. Well, she'd done it, taken what was probably a very dangerous step, possibly even a fatal one. She just didn't care. The heady lure of adventure had simply overpowered her need for safety.

Besides, she wasn't a naïve, gullible young girl. She could take care of herself. It would be like a game. Knowing Nick, his sense of his own importance and the authority he wielded over her, he probably figured he could just order her into bed.

She giggled a little hysterically at the thought. She could almost hear that imperious voice in its familiar commanding tone: All right, McIntyre, get your clothes off.

Well, we'll just see about that. He'd made it clear that their personal involvement would have no bearing on her job. She had nothing whatever to lose, and she could have a lot of fun.

Then she leapt to her feet, stricken, as a sudden terrible thought crossed her mind. She had absolutely nothing to wear!

The first thing next morning, as soon as the stores were open, Regan went shopping. Last evening she'd given a lot of thought to creating a brand new image. In a sense, she and Nick would be meeting for the first time tonight, at any rate on an entirely new footing, and first impressions were crucial.

The slinky rust-coloured dress she'd worn at the party in San Francisco wouldn't do, nor would the elaborate hairstyle with its stiff curls. He's said she looked like a streetwalker. She'd aim for elegance, something like the svelte blonde at that same party.

To achieve elegance, one had to be prepared to pay for it. She was earning a good salary and spent very little, so had accumulated a tidy bank balance. If she was going to have an adventure, she might as well do it right.

At nine o'clock, then, she entered the doors of a small exclusive boutique in the Broadway district of Capitol Hill that catered to some of the city's fashionable young society matrons, and put herself in the hands of an intelligent saleswoman who seemed to grasp immediately the kind of image Regan wanted to project.

She emerged two hours later, somewhat dazed, her arms laden with parcels, and several hundred dollars poorer.

But she'd achieved her goal, and, when she opened her door to Nick that evening at seven o'clock precisely, the look in his eyes when he saw her was reward enough for the money she'd spent and the agonies of apprehension she'd gone through that day getting ready for him.

The dress she'd chosen was a beautifully cut tissue *faille* in the palest yellow. It was the kind of dress that looked plain, even dowdy, on the hanger, but fitted so perfectly and was put together so cleverly that it made her feel every bit as elegant as she'd hoped. It was simplicity itself, with a fitted bodice, a wide, square neckline, small cap sleeves and tiny pleats at the waist that tapered down into a slim skirt.

Instead of tucking her thick shoulder-length brown hair behind her ears, as she usually did, she'd brushed until it gleamed, then let it hang loose to frame her face in soft waves. Another assistant at the shop had advised her about make-up, which was as subdued as the dress, and aimed particularly at emphasising her deep brown eyes.

When she heard his knock, she gave herself one last glance in the mirror in the hall, went to the door, stood there for a moment trying to compose herself, then opened it to him.

'Hello, Nick,' she said. She opened the door a little wider. 'Come on in.'

He gave her one long appraising look from under half-shut eyelids, then, as his gaze moved swiftly over her from head to her toes, he smiled a slow, intimate smile.

'Well,' he said with feeling, and stepped inside.

When she'd closed the door behind him, she turned to see that he was still looking at her intently. It took enormous effort to keep her hands still under that steady frankly appraising gaze. She kept having to remind herself not to fiddle with her face, her dress, her hair. Somehow his very presence made her so nervous that she could scarcely stand still. And the way he was *staring* at her! Those gimlet grey eyes seemed to be boring a hole right through her.

'You look very lovely tonight, Regan,' he said at last, moving a step towards her.

She couldn't help it, couldn't stop herself from raising a hand to her hair to smooth it back behind

her ears. Then she remembered just in time that she
wasn't wearing it that way tonight, that she mustn't
fidget. She must appear poised, calm, in control.

'Thank you,' she murmured.

He looked so wonderful himself, with his crisp
lightweight dark suit, white shirt and tie, that she
couldn't keep her eyes off him. He seemed different
tonight, and not at all what she was used to. It seemed
strange to have him actually inside her apartment at
all. The only other time he'd been there, they'd stayed
out in the corridor.

'I'm afraid I can't offer you a drink,' she said,
trying to keep the quaver out of her voice.

'That's all right. We should be going anyway. I
made our reservations for seven-thirty. Do you have
a wrap?'

'No. It's so nice out, I don't think I'll need one.'

He opened the door for her, and they stepped out
into the hall. Just as Regan finished locking it, there
came a clatter on the stairs and Don came bounding
down them. When he saw them standing there, he
slowed his pace.

'Hi, Regan,' he said. 'It looks as though you're
going out.'

'Yes,' she replied, flustered. 'We're just on our way
to dinner. Did you want something?'

'Oh, I just got an unexpected night off and came
down to see if you wanted to go out for a bite to eat.'
He gave Nick a quick sideways glance. 'But I see
you're busy.'

'I'm sorry, Don,' she said. 'Some other time.' She
looked nervously from Don to Nick. There couldn't
possibly be two men more different. 'Er—Nick, this

is Don Jameson, from upstairs. Don, Nick Wainwright.'

The two men nodded at each other, but neither made a move to shake hands. Don's were stuck in the back pockets of his shabby jeans, and Nick's hung loosely at his sides. They were eyeing each other so warily that any minute Regan expected them to start prowling around like stalking animals defending their territory.

'Well,' she said brightly. 'I guess we'd better be on our way. I'll see you later, Don.'

As she and Nick walked off down the hall together, she could sense Don watching after them every step of the way. What an awkward situation! She felt she should somehow explain to Nick that Don was only a friend, a neighbour, but he was so silent on the way downstairs that she didn't quite know how to broach the subject.

By the time they reached his sleek silver grey Mercedes, which was parked at the kerb in front of her building, she was glad she hadn't bothered to clarify her relationship with Don. It wouldn't hurt to let him think another man was interested in her.

When they were inside the car, and he'd started the engine, he turned to her before backing out of the parking space.

'I didn't realise the boyfriend lived in the same building with you,' he said casually.

'The boyfriend?' she asked.

'Wasn't he the one who drove you to the airport when we went to San Francisco?'

'Oh, yes. I'd forgotten.'

'I don't like to tread on another man's territory,' he remarked as he slid the car deftly out into the flow of traffic.

Regan bridled. 'I'm not anyone's "territory",' she said tartly. 'I'm a person.'

'Ah, yes,' he said with a smile. 'I forgot. You're a liberated woman.'

She wrinkled her nose with distaste. 'I hate that term,' she said. 'It sounds so... Oh, I don't know. So *aggressive*, somehow. I guess I just don't like labels.'

'Like male chauvinist pig?' he asked in a teasing tone. 'Nor do I. Let's just be Regan and Nick tonight and see where that takes us. Agreed?'

'Agreed,' she replied.

He took her to a waterfront restaurant on Shilshole Bay. The sun was still shining when they arrived, and from their table by a window they could watch the boats passing by on their way from the locks, the quicksilver flash of the salmon as they leapt in the air.

'How is the trial going?' she asked over drinks.

'We haven't really got moving on it yet, and the preliminaries are always rather tedious in any case,' he said. 'But let's not talk shop. I like to forget my work when I'm out for pleasure.' He put his elbows on the table, leaned towards her and gave her another of those warm, intimate smiles. 'Tell me about yourself, Regan. In spite of sharing a hotel suite with you for almost a week, I actually know very little about you.'

It was on the tip of her tongue to remind him that was because he'd virtually ignored her that whole week except to bark orders at her, but she stopped herself just in time. If he didn't want to discuss business this evening, neither did she.

'What do you want to know?' she asked.

He laughed. 'This isn't a job interview. I just want to find out more about you, as a person. A woman,' he added softly.

She was still having trouble adjusting to this new Nick. She'd become so accustomed to the brusque, impatient, authoritative image he'd projected on the job that it was hard to relate to him in this brand new role. Who was the real Nick Wainwright? The old tyrant, or this warm, courteous, apparently caring man?

She began to tell him about her background, that she'd been born and raised in Yakima, that her mother had died when she was twelve, leaving her father to raise her and her two sisters alone, his insistence that she go on to law school after college.

He kept questioning her all through dinner, expertly, almost as though demonstrating his famous courtroom tactics, but apparently with genuine interest, and when, over their after-dinner coffee, she told him the story of her father's obsession with Shakespeare, he threw back his head and laughed aloud.

'So that's how you got your name,' he remarked. He shook his head slowly from side to side. 'I'd like to meet your father. A man so enamoured of the Bard that he'd name his children after King Lear's daughters has got to be a man of character and imagination.'

'That's easy for you to say,' she commented drily. 'You're not the one who has to do all the explaining.'

'Yes,' he agreed. 'I can imagine that must have led you into more than one sticky situation.'

After dinner he excused himself to go to the men's room, and, as she watched him walk off, tall, strong, dashing in his dark suit, his gait graceful and assured, she suddenly realised that she was having a very good time. He was wonderful company, and the skilful way he'd drawn her out was really rather flattering.

Alone at the table, however, without his over-whelming presence, she was reminded with a little shock just who she was dealing with here. The Nick Wainwright she knew was *not* kind and warm and courteous, he was the scourge of the legal profession in general, and the law firm she worked for in particular.

It was then she began to have qualms about what lay ahead that evening. What would he expect in payment for all that flattery and attention? He was not a man to take a refusal meekly, like Don Jameson. Would she have to beat him off?

Once again the image arose in her mind of that late-night encounter in the hotel suite in San Francisco, and a sudden rush of warmth began to course through her at the memory. Did she really want to beat him off? What would it be like to have a full-blown affair with a man like Nick?

She looked up to see him making his way back to the table just then, and quickly put such dangerous thoughts out of her mind. It was tempting, but out of the question. If he did get amorous, she'd just have to let him know, kindly but firmly, that she had no intention of becoming one of his easy conquests.

'Would you like an after-dinner drink?' he asked when he'd sat down. 'Some brandy?'

'No,' she said. 'Nothing for me.'

'If you don't mind, I think I will.'

He hailed a passing waiter and ordered a glass of cognac. When it came he lit a thin brown cheroot, leaned back in his chair and puffed contentedly.

Regan put an elbow on the table and rested her chin in her hand. 'You've quizzed me all evening,' she said. 'What about you?'

'Me? There's not much to tell. I have a very dull background.'

'I can't believe that.'

'All right. Take a guess, then. What kind of roots do you think I've sprung from?'

'Let's see,' she mused. She thought a moment. 'I know. You were an orphan who made his way to the top after a heroic struggle with poverty and hardship.'

He smiled and shook his head. 'Nope.'

'Well, then, you were the only child of wealthy parents who indulged your every whim and spoiled you rotten.'

He laughed explosively at that. 'Wrong again. All right, if you insist. The truth is, I come from a very close, very normal, rather large family. Two brothers and three sisters. Six nieces and nephews at last count. Parents still living in the old place in the Madrona district. Grew up right here in Seattle. Did all the things most kids do, played a little football in high school, did average in college, then caught fire when I began to study law.'

She could only goggle at him, hardly able to believe he was telling her the truth. It wasn't at all the romantic background she had pictured for him.

He was eyeing her with amusement, his thin mouth curled in a gently mocking smile, the little lines at the corners of his eyes crinkled. 'You do have a fertile imagination, my girl,' he said admiringly. 'Must have inherited it from your Shakespeare-loving father.'

'I'm just surprised, that's all.' Then she laughed. 'You were right. It does sound rather dull.'

When he'd finished his brandy and cigar and paid the bill, they went out into the car park in front of the restaurant. It was quite dark by now, but still balmy, with a gentle breeze blowing off Puget Sound, the sound of lapping waves drifting up from the shore below.

Inside the car, he started the engine, then turned to her. 'It's such a lovely evening. Would you like to go for a short drive? I'll show you where I live.'

She hesitated for a moment, then said, 'All right. Sounds nice.'

Once again her curiosity had triumphed over her common sense. She was dying to see where he lived. There was nothing that said she had to go inside, or even get out of the car. Although she still sensed danger from him, he certainly wasn't the kind of man to drag her bodily into his den and overpower her.

Besides, it was quite pleasant, even exhilarating, to be driven through the city streets at night in a powerful car by a man like Nick. From time to time as they drove she would dart little sideways glances at his profile, silhouetted against the street lights. She decided that, while his fine straight nose was still his best feature, the rest of him was not bad at all.

In fact, now that she'd seen this entirely new side of him, he'd begun to seem downright handsome to her. There was a rugged sense of power and quick energy about him, an aura of authority that was intensely appealing. Everything he did was graceful and assured, and to have caught a glimpse of his softer side tonight only enhanced that appeal.

At the entrance to the motorway he pulled on to a northbound ramp, and before long they exited at the small town of Edmonds. As he negotiated through the narrow streets heading west towards the beach, he kept up a chatty commentary on the history of the area, which had started as a small fishing village and was now on the fringes of Seattle's urban sprawl.

As they approached the ferry terminal, Regan wondered if his intention was to take her on a late-night ride across Puget Sound to one of the islands, but at the last city street he turned north again, and soon they were climbing a steep hill towards a prom-ontory that jutted out over the small harbour.

He turned into a wide paved avenue of large houses facing the water, and, although it was dark out, there was enough glow from the street lights and front garden lamps to reveal the opulence of the neigh-bourhood. At the end of the street, he pulled up at the kerb of a low rambling redwood structure set well back on a large plot of woodsy grounds.

'Well,' he said, turning to her. 'This is it. Home sweet home.' He switched off the engine.

Regan peered out of the window. 'It looks quite imposing.'

He shrugged. 'It's all right. I only wish I had more time to spend in it.' Then, in a light casual tone, he said, 'How about a personally conducted tour?'

Alarm bells went off in Regan's head. Fun was fun, and a game was a game, but she wasn't quite ready to take it as far as a seduction attempt on their first night out. It had been a very enjoyable evening. She didn't want to spoil it, but if the relationship was to continue she had to keep the upper hand. Once he took control, she'd be lost.

'It's getting late,' she said quite firmly. 'Maybe some other time.'

Immediately, and without comment or argument, he switched on the engine, made a U-turn and headed back in the direction he'd come.

All the way back to her apartment, he continued discussing local trivia in the same conversational tone as before. If he was annoyed or put off by her refusal, he gave no indication of it, and Regan had to admire his aplomb. A lesser man would have kept trying, but he seemed to accept it with such good grace that she had to wonder if she'd been mistaken, even half regretted not letting him show her his house. It might have been her last chance.

After he'd parked in front of her place, he got out and opened the car door for her, then walked up with her to her apartment and waited while she got out her key. After unlocking the door, she turned to him to say goodnight.

'Thank you for a lovely evening, Nick,' she said politely. 'I enjoyed the dinner very much, and the ride.'

'My pleasure,' he said with a brief nod.

Then, before she had any idea what his intentions were, he had bent down swiftly, put a hand lightly on her cheek and brushed her lips with his own, his mouth lingering there just long enough to let her know it was definitely not just a friendly kiss, but withdrawing before it became frankly amorous.

'I'll call you in the morning,' he said as he drew away from her.

The next thing she knew he had dropped his hand from her face, turned away and set off down the hall. Still reeling from the impact of that unexpected kiss, she slowly pushed the door open. Inside, she closed it behind her, then leaned back against it with her eyes shut tight. She put her fingers to her lips. She could still taste his mouth, the brandy he'd had after dinner, the cheroot he'd smoked, and still smell his particular masculine scent.

Her head spun dizzily. He said he'd call her tomorrow. What did it all mean? A faint inner voice warned her that she was fast on the way to getting in over her head, but the prospect was so tempting that she didn't even care.

The next morning, just as she was finishing breakfast and still mulling over the events of the night before, there came a knock on her door. She ran to answer it, glancing at her watch on the way. It was only nine o'clock.

'Yes,' she called. 'Who is it?'

'Regan McIntyre?' came a loud masculine voice.

'Yes.'

'Delivery for you.'

With the chain bolt still attached, she opened the door a crack and saw a young boy standing there holding a long florist's box. She undid the chain and took the box from him, then thanked him before he scurried off down the hall, whistling under his breath.

She ran into the kitchen, set the box on the counter and tore off the lid. There, nestled inside on layers of green tissue paper, were masses of long-stemmed pale yellow roses. They were lightly scented, and she gasped aloud at their beauty. The sheer quantity of them was overwhelming.

There was a small white card lying on top. She picked it up and read the short message in Nick's familiar masculine scrawl.

> 'These seemed to match the colour of the dress you wore last night, but don't nearly do justice to the lady wearing it.'

Just then the telephone rang, and she almost tripped running to answer it. Her heart was thudding so hard that she was afraid she wouldn't be able to speak, and she made herself stop for a few seconds in the hallway before lifting the receiver.

Then slowly she picked it up and said hello.

'Good morning,' came Nick's cheery voice. 'Did you get the flowers?'

'Yes, they're absolutely gorgeous.' She laughed. 'How in the world did you manage to find a florist open so early, and on Sunday morning at that? Not to mention one who had roses just that colour.'

'Ah, I have my sources,' he said. 'I'm glad you liked them.'

'How could I help it? Thank you.'

'I called to see if you were up to a ride in the mountains today. They've just opened Salish Lodge, and I thought we could have a late lunch, say around two o'clock, then take a short walk to see the wild flowers. They're spectacular this time of year.'

Wild flowers? she thought. He was the last man in the world she would ever have expected to be interested in wild flowers.

'Yes,' she replied promptly. 'I'd like that.'

'Wear something for walking in, then, and I'll pick you up around one o'clock.'

After a delightful day in the mountains, he dropped her off early that evening at her place, since they both had to work the next day.

During the day he'd been good company, and, even though they'd hiked some distance from the lodge to an isolated spot, he'd never once touched her, except to take her hand or arm once or twice to help her over a particularly rocky terrain.

At her door he repeated his performance of the night before, only this time his hand on her cheek slid around to grasp the back of her neck, pulling her more closely towards him, and his lips lingered a little longer on hers, pulling at them gently, seductively. Then, once again, he said goodnight, turned and walked away from her.

The minute she got inside, she was greeted by the scent of the roses sitting on the coffee-table in her living-room. Somehow the sight of them made her wish she'd had the nerve to invite Nick inside. Those brief kisses of his were beginning to leave her vaguely dissatisfied, restless, and definitely longing for more.

During the following week they saw each other every night, and it was always the same. He took her out to dinner, to a movie, to the opening of an art gallery in Pioneer Square, to a jazz concert, even to an opera. His tastes seemed to be eclectic and varied, but since all she cared about was being with him she didn't really care what they did.

Every evening when he took her home, the same routine was repeated. He never asked to come in, he always left her at the door, and although his kisses and caresses grew increasingly exploratory and ardent, he always left her just short of what she hoped for.

All during that week at work, she went out of her way to avoid him, and especially stayed away from the coffee-room, which was on the same floor as his office. It gave her a pleasant conspiratorial feeling to know he was in the same building, just one floor below, and she hugged this knowledge to herself like a guilty secret.

On Friday, however, Jim Courtney sent her down to the library on a special errand, and she had to venture downstairs, like it or not. She crept down the steps feeling like a criminal, alert for any sign of him, as though just seeing each other would alert the whole office to the true nature of their relationship.

It was mid-morning, and since most of the lawyers took their break then the library was virtually empty. Laura was the only one there, hunched over a thick legal volume, looking miserable. When she raised her head and saw Regan, she frowned.

'Where have you been all week?' she demanded in a loud voice. 'Hiding out up there with your bank merger?'

Regan started guiltily. 'Yes,' she said hastily. 'That's it. Jim Courtney just sent me down now to do some research.'

Laura stretched widely and got up from her chair. 'Oh, you can take a few minutes for a break. There are some new developments in my love-life, and I need your advice.'

'My advice?' Regan said with a laugh. 'What do I know about it?'

'Oh, it's just that you're so level-headed,' Laura said. 'Come on. Five minutes.'

Regan was about to make some excuse when just at that moment Nick walked into the library. She grew warm all over just at the sight of him, but he, composed as always, merely nodded at the two women and strode directly over to the bookshelves.

Regan turned to Laura, hoping her confusion didn't show on her flaming face. 'All right,' she said in a low voice. 'I can take a few minutes.'

The coffee-room was just emptying out, and, after filling their cups, they sat down a vacant table. Laura immediately launched into a long story about how she'd decided to continue her affair with the married man in spite of the fact that he'd gone back to his wife, and Regan only half listened, still shaken by the encounter with Nick.

She was a little disturbed by his distant attitude towards her. He could have at least have smiled at her. She knew he was only being cautious, but it was so much like the old dictatorial days that it made their new more personal relationship seem like a dream.

Then she realised that Laura was peering at her intently. 'I'm sorry, Laura,' she said. 'I didn't quite catch that. What did you say?'

'Where is your mind?' Laura protested. 'I was asking you if you thought I was crazy to stick with Kevin now that he's decided to stay with his wife.'

'Honestly, Laura, I wish I could help you, but I'm the last person to give you advice about men. I guess you have to do what your instincts tell you to do and hope for the best.' She hastily downed her coffee and got up from her chair. 'Now I really have to get that research attended to.'

Nick was gone when she returned to the library. She found the volume she needed, and, as she pored over the legalities of Jim's merger, she thought about Laura and her romantic problems. Her own situation was so different, and she realised how lucky she was. Even if she and Nick had to hide their relationship, at least it wasn't because he was tied to another woman.

Saturday was to be their last night before he had to leave to go back to his trial in San Francisco. As Regan got ready early that evening, she tried not to think about it. Every time she did it brought on an unpleasant sinking sensation in the pit of her stomach. Would this be the last time she'd ever see him? Was it going to end before it really got started?

He still hadn't pressed her beyond that one goodnight kiss, and by now his delaying tactics were tormenting her with unfulfilled desire. She wished she'd had more experience with men than those few fumbling episodes in her college days.

The feeling she had for Nick was light years beyond anything she'd ever known before, and she simply wasn't equipped to handle it sensibly. By now she was already half in love with him, in way over her head, and although she knew that whatever control she'd had at the beginning was long gone, she had no idea what to do about it.

That night when he came to get her, he was unusually silent all the way down to the car. Before starting the engine he turned to her with a grave expression on his face, then reached out for her hand and clasped it between both of his.

'I'm leaving tomorrow, you know,' he said softly.

She nodded. 'I know.'

Raising her hand to his lips, he looked directly into her eyes. 'I don't know when I'll be able to get back. I'll try to make it on the weekends, but it'll depend largely on how the trial goes.'

She nodded again. 'Yes,' she said, forcing out a smile.

One of his hands had moved to the base of her throat now, caressing her gently, the long fingers moving on her skin. The sensations that touch was arousing in her almost choked her. She could scarcely breathe.

Without shifting his gaze from hers, he smiled crookedly. 'Since it's our last night, then, I thought you might like to have dinner at my place rather than going out to a restaurant.'

She didn't even hesitate. 'Yes,' she replied. 'I'd like that.'

His whole face lit up, but all he did was nod. Slowly he withdrew his hands and turned to start the car.

All the way out they made small talk, speaking in short stilted sentences. The powerful electric tension inside the car virtually crackled between them, and Regan wondered if he felt it too. Her stomach seemed to be on a roller-coaster, rising up into her throat, then plunging down again.

Although she was apprehensive about what lay ahead that evening, she knew she had to go through with it. She had no choice. All she could do was follow her instincts and hope for the best.

CHAPTER SEVEN

THE minute they were inside the large cool tiled entrance hall of his house, Nick turned to Regan and took her in his arms. With a sigh, she leaned towards him, and when their lips met at last, a shower of sparks seemed to burst inside her head. The pressure of his kiss was firm, but not urgent, and after a few moments he moved his lips to her ear.

'Mmm,' he murmured. 'I've been waiting to do this all week.'

She drew her head back and looked up at him. 'Well, why didn't you?' she asked.

He grinned down at her. 'I didn't want to scare you off. You shied away so quickly the first night I brought you out here, that I was afraid if I pushed you'd bolt altogether and I'd never get another chance.'

'Well . . .' she said hesitantly.

'That's all right,' he assured her. He pulled her a little tighter. 'I don't like my women too easy.'

There was something about his tone of voice, the words themselves, that she found vaguely disturbing. He made it sound too much like a game. To her it was a powerful mutual attraction that neither of them could resist. She put her hands on his forearms, moved back a step and gave him a cool smile.

'I thought you were going to give me a tour of the house,' she said. 'Hadn't we better do that while it's still light?'

He narrowed his eyes at her for a moment, then nodded. 'All right. The grand tour it'll be.'

As he took her around from room to room, Regan became so entranced with the house that her uneasiness gradually faded. The large tiled entrance led into an enormous living-room with a rough stone fireplace at one end. The long wall facing the water was entirely made of glass panels, with bamboo blinds half drawn against the sun.

It was a very masculine house, with cool greys and blues predominating, and furnished sparsely with sturdy-looking chairs and tables. His bedroom was large and roomy, but almost monk-like in its simplicity. There were two other bedrooms, both with their own baths, a formal dining-room and a comfortable library with another fireplace that was furnished almost exactly like his office.

As they went from room to room he explained that he'd had it custom-built to his exact plans and specifications by a well-known local architect just two years ago, and that it was the house he'd dreamed of owning ever since he could remember. Every nook and cranny of it seemed to reflect his unique personality. There was a feeling of spaciousness about it, of freedom, that was just like his own independent, rather lonely nature.

After they'd finished exploring the interior, Nick stopped in the kitchen to fix a drinks tray, and they went out on to the terrace. When he'd filled their glasses with potent martinis, they settled down in comfortably cushioned redwood chairs gazing out at the Sound, the city, the mountains in the distant background.

'It's a wonderful house, Nick,' she said. 'I can see why you love it so much.'

He shrugged. 'It's inconvenient in a way, living clear out here. Commuting is the very devil, especially in the wintertime, but I got fed up with apartment living in the city after ten years of it. I needed room to breathe, fresh air.'

'I know what you mean,' she said with a little sigh. 'I get to feeling pretty cramped in my place, too.'

He smiled at her. 'Well, now that you're going to be a rich lawyer, you'll be able to afford a house of your own some day.'

She laughed. 'Well, I can dream, can't I?'

He drained the last of his martini, rose to his feet and stood before her. 'Would you like another drink?'

She glanced up at him. 'No thanks. They're pretty strong. One is more than enough for me.'

'Then I think I'll go stick our dinner in the oven.' He braced his hands on the wide wooden arms of her chair, then leaned down and brushed his mouth briefly over hers. 'Don't go away.'

After he'd gone into the house, Regan walked over to the edge of the sloping lawn and stood there gazing out at the spectacular view. The sun had just gone down behind the mountains, and the lights of the city were twinkling in the gathering dusk.

Neither she nor Nick had made any reference to the scene in the hall when they'd first arrived, and by now she was feeling a little silly at her reaction to his remark. It hadn't been *that* offensive. It was only his way.

In a few minutes she heard the door to the house close and his slow footsteps coming towards her on the paved terrace. Finally he stopped directly behind her. His arms came around her, and as she leaned back against him, he lifted the thick hair from her shoulders and pressed his lips on her neck.

'Turn around,' he said.

Slowly, she turned to see him looking down at her, his expression grave. Their eyes met and locked together for several long seconds. Then he reached out for her, and the next thing she knew she was in his arms.

As his head bent down, she raised her arms up around his neck and closed her eyes. He tightened his hold on her, and when his seeking mouth settled on hers all her doubts about the wisdom of what she was doing fled from her mind.

This was all that mattered, to be held in his arms, to breathe in the masculine scent of him, the taste of his mouth, to feel the hard body pressed against her own. She slid her hands over the back of his neck to rake her fingers through the smooth black hair, then dropped her head back as his mouth left hers and moved down over her chin, her neck, to settle on her throat.

With one arm still tightly holding her around the waist, his other hand travelled around over her ribcage and across her waist, then moved slowly upward to cover her breasts, moving from one to the other in slow lazy strokes that set her pulses racing, her heart pounding, a distant ringing sensation in her ears.

'I want you, Regan,' he murmured against her mouth. 'I've wanted you for a long time, ever since that one crazy midnight in San Francisco. Say you want me, too.'

She could scarcely breathe. 'Oh, yes,' she choked out.

With a low groan of satisfaction deep in his throat, his mouth opened wider, his tongue thrust past her lips, and at the same time the hand at her breast slipped inside the neckline of her white silk shirt to clasp the bare soft flesh underneath. His fingers began to make slow circles around the taut peak, teasing gently, sending shafts of fire flickering through her already heated bloodstream.

Suddenly he tore his mouth from hers and drew slightly away from her. Feeling chilled, Regan opened her eyes to see him pulling off his tie, undoing the top button of his white shirt. Then, slowly, he reached for the opening of her blouse.

She started to tremble. This was what she wanted, what she had known was coming. He had already aroused her to a feverish pitch of desire, and there was no turning back now. When she felt his fingers working at the buttons of her shirt, his hands brushing against her breasts as they moved lower, she closed her eyes and fought down the panicky feeling that was rising up inside her.

Just then from inside the house came the ringing of a telephone. Regan's eyes flew open. She looked down. Nick already had three buttons of her shirt undone and was working on the fourth.

'The telephone,' she murmured.

'Never mind,' he said. His even white teeth flashed in a warm intimate smile. 'I've got more important things on my mind at the moment.'

The jangling noise kept on and on, jarring at her nerves. She placed her hand over his, stilling it. The telephone stopped ringing just then, but the spell was broken. That sudden interruption had spoiled the mood, and, as sanity returned, Regan realised that she was getting into something she wasn't prepared to deal with, not yet.

She looked at Nick. He had dropped his hands and was resting them on his narrow hips, gazing at her through half-closed lids.

'What's wrong, Regan?' he asked quietly.

Clutching nervously at the opening of her blouse, she turned away from him and started redoing the buttons. When she was presentable, she turned back to him and gave him a tremulous smile.

'I'm not sure,' she said in a shaky voice. 'I think maybe I'm not quite ready for this. I mean,' she faltered, 'shouldn't we at least discuss the way we feel about each other before...?' She broke off and waved a hand helplessly in the air.

He gazed at her speculatively for several seconds. Then his mouth curled in a slightly mocking smile. He ran a hand over his smooth dark hair and stooped down to pick up the tie he'd dropped on the terrace. He slung it loosely around his neck, and when he faced her again the grey eyes were stony.

'Let's go sit down,' he said brusquely.

He started walking away from her. She watched as he stopped at the low table between their chairs, poured himself another drink and downed half of it in one gulp. She went back to her chair and sat stiffly on the very edge of the cushion, waiting.

He came over to sit opposite her, carrying his glass. 'I think we need to have a little talk,' he said quietly.

Regan braced herself. 'What about?'

He sipped meditatively at his drink for a moment, then said, 'I like you, Regan, I really do. In fact, you're the first woman I've ever worked with who has interested me even slightly, and it took a hell of a lot of fancy mental footwork for me to convince myself it would work at all.'

Regan waited. She knew there was more coming. A lot more.

'But I'm not a boy. I'm thirty-seven years old, and, as much as I like you, as much as I'm attracted to you, I think it would be a waste of time for us both to fool around with a lot of boring adolescent preliminaries if it's not going to lead anywhere.'

He paused then and took another swallow of his drink, watching her over the rim of the glass as though waiting for her to speak.

Regan was totally confused by his words. Was he talking about a serious commitment? Marriage? She hardly dared hope. Finally, as the silence lengthened, she knew she had to say something.

'I'm not sure I understand what you mean,' she said steadily.

He sighed. 'Let me put it this way. It's been my experience that women aren't as interested these days in marriage and a family as they used to be.' He paused for a second, but when she remained silent, went on, 'In any case, I think you need to know that those things are not on the cards for me, and, since I realise how important your career is to you, I naturally assumed you felt the same way.'

Regan's heart sank. That wasn't at all what she'd hoped to hear, and his blunt statement threw her completely off base.

'Why are you telling me this?' she asked, stalling for time.

'The way you keep running hot and cold bothers me, that's all. You're like a damned yo-yo. We're adults, Regan, and we both have work we're committed to. I'm not interested in playing children's games. Either we're attracted enough to each other to do something about it, or we aren't.'

'I see.' Now that he'd set forth his brilliant theories so clearly, she was beginning to find his easy assumptions about their future extremely annoying. 'Let me see if I have this straight. You're saying that if I'm not willing to have an affair with you there's no point in our seeing each other any more.'

To her satisfaction a deep red flush washed over his face. 'That's putting it rather bluntly, but, yes, that's pretty much what I have on my mind.'

'And you mean right now, I take it,' she said in a dry sarcastic tone. 'Tonight. This minute.'

He frowned heavily. 'Now you're only being difficult. If I've offended you, I'm sorry,' he went on stiffly. 'I'm only trying to be honest with you.'

She settled back in her chair and gave him a long cool look. His obvious loss of composure was intensely satisfying to her. She seemed to be the one in control now, and she felt a surge of reckless confidence. She had nothing to lose at this point anyway.

'Oh, I appreciate that,' she said in a slow drawling tone. 'But I am curious about one thing.'

'What's that?'

'Last week when you told me about your family background, you made it sound so wonderful, so warm and close and loving, that I can't help wondering what soured you on marriage?'

'All right,' he replied promptly. 'I'll tell you. Actually, I have the highest regard for the institution itself. In fact, I live the way I do *because* I have so much respect for family life.' He was warming to his subject now, his voice rising heatedly. 'But I've seen too many two-career marriages with children parked in day-care centres, husbands and wives hardly ever seeing each other, going off on business trips with co-workers of the opposite sex, and I decided long ago that I won't have any part of it.'

'I see. You're assuming all women put careers before family, then.' She laughed harshly. 'It sounds a lot to me like your old paranoia about liberated women at work here.'

'You're quite mistaken,' he said tersely. 'As a matter of fact men have actually gained enormous advantages from feminism. I've just given up expecting to find a real woman.'

'And what do you call a "real" woman?'

'I can't define it precisely, but I know I'd recognise one if I saw her. And I certainly recognise the ones who are only imitation men.' He made an impatient gesture with his hand. 'Come on, Regan, let's quit this sparring around. I'm not trying to be offensive, only truthful. I've told you I'm attracted to you. I think you're attracted to me. And if you were honest with yourself, I think you'd admit that, as a career woman yourself, the last thing in the world you want is to be tied to a husband and children.'

Just then a loud buzzer sounded, and he rose to his feet. 'Come on,' he said. 'Our dinner is ready.'

An hour later, they sat at the counter in his spacious, well-equipped kitchen finishing up their meal, a crab casserole, green salad and thick slices of sourdough French bread.

The bone of contention between them hadn't been mentioned again. Nick seemed to be deliberately avoiding the subject, and Regan didn't have the nerve to raise it again. In fact, watching him now as he sat opposite her, she was already deeply regretting her rejection of his lovemaking. If only she weren't so attracted to him! She cared too much for him to let him go so easily.

And tomorrow he'd leave. Already she could see the familiar signs that he was thinking about his work, not her. There was an air of distraction about him, as though he weren't really there with her at all. Although they'd chatted easily about how he'd come to build his house and the trials and tribulations of the construction, the silences between became longer and longer.

'I had no idea you could cook,' Regan said brightly at last.

He gave her a quick smile. 'I can't. I have a talented young Vietnamese couple who take care of all my domestic needs.'

'Lucky you.'

There was another long silence, while Nick gazed abstractedly into the distance, eating mechanically, his mind obviously a million miles away. He looked tired, too.

Regan finished the last bite of crab on her plate and slid off her stool. 'I'll just do up these dishes,' she said.

'No. Don't bother. Mung will take care of that tomorrow when he comes to clean up and help me get my things ready to pack.'

'Oh. Well, then, I suppose it's time I was getting home.' She'd been hoping against hope that he'd try again, but now she knew it wasn't going to happen. 'You probably have a lot to do tomorrow, and it's getting late.'

'Yes,' he said. 'My plane leaves early tomorrow evening, and I still have to get my papers in order.'

'Well, then, I'll just get my bag.'

They hardly spoke at all on the way to her place. The traffic on the freeway was unusually heavy, even for a Saturday night, and Nick focused all his attention on his driving.

Regan sat miserably beside him, sunk in gloom at the prospect of not seeing him for lord knew how long. The delicious dinner she'd eaten sat like a lump of lead in her stomach, and she only hoped she could make it to her place without disgracing herself by bursting into tears or begging for another chance.

At her place, he walked to her door with her, as usual, then leaned down and gave her a brief peck on the forehead, but she could tell that his heart wasn't in it. It was almost like a duty he was performing, as though it was expected of him.

'I don't know when I'll get back,' he said distantly. 'You know how these things are.'

She smiled at him. 'Yes. Of course. Well, good luck. I hope it goes well for you down there.'

'Thanks. I'll try to call you later in the week and let you know my plans.'

'Good. I'd like that.'

'Well, goodnight, then, Regan.'

'Goodnight, Nick.'

He turned and walked away from her, and she hurried inside to the safety of her own apartment. She couldn't bear to see him actually leaving. Throwing her bag down on the couch in the living-room, she ran into her bedroom, threw herself down on the bed, and allowed the pent-up tears to flow at last.

The next few weeks were the hardest Regan had ever lived through. The boredom and loneliness she'd experienced before Nick came into her life now seemed like child's play compared to the agony of waiting by the telephone every night hoping he'd call, and, when, after two weeks, he hadn't, the even worse pain of regret that she'd been fool enough to let him go so easily.

As she plodded through her boring contracts and deeds at the office, or listlessly performed the usual weekend chores in her apartment, she could hardly believe how keenly she felt his absence. They'd known each other such a short time, really, only a couple of months. He'd entered her life like a whirlwind, his dynamic presence taking it over so completely that her existence seemed empty without him.

She thought about him constantly. At night, lying in bed, she tormented herself with visions of elegant blondes hanging all over him down there in San Francisco. At the office she kept expecting to see him in the corridors, the library, the coffee-room, hoping just to hear someone mention his name, but it was as though he'd disappeared from the face of the earth.

The only real social life she could tolerate was with Don Jameson, but he worked such odd long hours at the hospital that she only saw him rarely. Although she found his cheerful company oddly soothing, it was only as a friend. He didn't arouse the remotest trace of passion in her. Not like Nick.

It was late July, the days warm and sunny, the evenings pleasant even after sundown. One Thursday night, just after she came home from work, she was standing in her kitchen thinking her dreary thoughts and wondering what in the world to have for dinner, when Don himself appeared at her door wearing his usual grubby clothes.

'Good,' he said, giving her a lopsided grin. 'You're home. Let's go.'

She stared at him. 'Go where?'

'I've got the night off and thought you might want to help me celebrate. We can pick up a pizza and some beer and have ourselves a picnic supper in the park at Green Lake.'

'Oh, I don't know, Don,' she replied. 'I'm kind of tired. It's been a rotten week, and I have to be at work early tomorrow morning.' She made a face. 'Another dull meeting with my bankers.'

Don cocked his head to one side and eyed her sternly. 'You're not tired,' he pronounced in firm tones. 'You're just bored.'

She shrugged. 'I won't argue with that. But it amounts to pretty much the same thing, doesn't it?'

'No, it doesn't. I'm the doctor, remember? Trust me. What I prescribe is a change of scene. Now, go change your clothes and let's get going.'

'Oh, all right,' she said with a laugh. 'You win. You're probably right. Come on in. I'll only be a minute.'

While Don waited for her in the living-room, Regan went to her bedroom to change. Don was right. She was bored, and not just from the stupid bank merger. It would do her good to get out of that depressing apartment. By the time she'd shed her lightweight tan poplin suit and put on a pair of jeans and a cotton shirt, she was already feeling much better.

She hung up her suit, tucked her hair back behind her ears, and went back out into the living-room.

'OK,' she said, retrieving her handbag from the couch where she'd dropped it. 'All ready.'

'My, that was quick,' Don commented with a grin.

They started towards the door, and, just as they reached it, the telephone began to ring. Regan stopped short. She was tempted not to answer it. Then she heaved a sigh and crossed over to the table in the hall where it sat.

'Just a second, Don. I'd better get that. It could be Jim Courtney, or possibly my father.'

She lifted the receiver and said hello.

'Regan? It's Nick.'

Her heart began to thud erratically and her knees almost buckled under her as the strange sensation of giddiness she always experienced at the sound of his voice hit her. Clutching the receiver tightly in her hand, she glanced over at Don. He was standing with his back to her, his hands in his pockets, looking out of the window.

'How are you?' she said to Nick, striving for a casual tone.

'Working hard. How about you?'

There was an unfamiliar note of caution in his voice, almost as though he was testing the waters. He actually sounded nervous, dubious about her reception of his call, even unsure of himself for the first time in living memory.

'Yes,' she said. 'Me, too. We've been pretty busy. The bank merger is about ready for final signature, and there are always a lot of last minute changes to be made. How's the trial going?'

'It's moving right along.'

There was a silence on the line then. Regan couldn't think of a single thing to say. She wanted to ask him why he had called, but Don's presence made conversation so awkward that she only waited, hardly daring to breathe.

'The reason I called,' he said at last, 'was to ask you to come down here for the weekend.'

The telephone receiver threatened to slip out of her clammy hand, and she got a firmer grip on it. 'What for?' she asked in a tight voice.

'I want to see you,' he replied slowly. There was another short silence, and she heard him clear his throat before going on. 'It's been bothering me, the way we left things the last time we saw each other, and I guess I was—well—hoping that maybe you'd changed your mind. You know, about . . .' His voice trailed off.

Regan could hardly believe her ears. This couldn't be the Nick Wainwright she knew. He was actually stumbling over his words. She thought fast. Before she could decide, she had to know what he meant by this unexpected request.

'Just what did you have in mind?' she asked cautiously.

'The judge has called a recess for Monday, and I've made reservations at a small lodge on the coast at Carmel. It's lovely there this time of year. If you could fly down tomorrow night, we'd have three full days together.'

Everything in Regan wanted to go. Of course she knew quite well what the implications were of that lodge at Carmel. This time it wouldn't be a suite. He was telling her he still wanted her. But not that his terms had altered. It was to be an affair—or nothing. Was she ready for that?

She couldn't think with Don in the room, listening to every word. She had to stall for time. 'Listen, Nick,' she said at last. 'There's someone here, and we're just on our way out. Can you call me back later? Say around ten o'clock?'

He hesitated for a moment. 'All right,' he agreed reluctantly. 'Ten o'clock.'

After they'd said goodbye, Regan carefully replaced the receiver, then turned around to face Don. He was watching her through half-closed eyes, a strange twisted smile on his face, his arms crossed over his chest.

'That sounded pretty heavy,' he commented lightly. 'Sorry, I couldn't help overhearing.'

She stared at him blankly, still in a daze. She'd managed to put Nick off for a few hours, but she still didn't know what to do. All of a sudden, she felt an urgent need to talk about it.

'That was Nick Wainwright,' she blurted. 'He wants me to go down to San Francisco this weekend.'

Don raised an eyebrow. 'Business?'

She shook her head slowly. 'No. Personal.' She started walking slowly towards him, wringing her hands as she went. 'I don't know what to do, Don,' she said when she reached him.

'Well, Regan,' he said slowly, 'I guess that all depends on what you *want* to do.'

She gave him a stricken look. 'What I *want* to do and what it's *right* to do are two different things.'

He shrugged his narrow shoulders. 'What can I say? From what I've seen and heard of the guy, it seems to me that you're only asking for trouble if you get

involved with him. But——' he gave her another
crooked smile '—I have to admit my motives are
personal.'

She turned from him and began pacing the room.
It had been a mistake to ask Don for advice. She'd
forgotten that he was interested in her himself.

'Regan,' she heard him say.

She turned around to face him. Why couldn't she
fall in love with him? Nice, safe, kind Don!

'Do you love him?' he asked carefully.

She nodded, shamefaced and miserable.

'Does he love you?'

'I don't think so,' she said in a small voice. Then
she heaved a deep sigh. 'That's not true. I *know* he
doesn't.'

'Well, look at it this way. If it's what you really
want, maybe you should go for it. Just so long as you
realise chances are a thousand to one you'll get hurt.'
His voice took on a harsher tone. 'You're not a naïve
young girl, after all. Maybe this is something you need
to get out of your system. You'll probably live through
it. Sadder and wiser, maybe, but you'll survive. And
who knows? I might still be there waiting in the wings
when it happens.'

She wanted to tell him that she was more inex-
perienced and naïve than he realised, but decided there
had been enough discussion of her personal life
already. Nick was going to call her back at ten o'clock.
Until then, she'd try to forget about it and hope that
it would somehow resolve itself.

She gave Don a bright smile. 'Come on. Let's go
get that pizza. I'm starved.'

* * *

After their picnic, they took a short walk around the south end of the lake, and Don dropped her off at her door just before nine o'clock. The subject of Nick Wainwright hadn't arisen again during the entire evening. Regan didn't want to discuss it any more, and Don seemed to sense her need for privacy.

When she was alone again in her own apartment, she went into the bathroom, ran a hot tub, and soaked in it until the water cooled. She still wasn't sure what her answer would be. It was as though she was waiting for a sign from heaven to guide her.

But none came. Her one consistent thought, overriding every other consideration, was that she wanted to go. Don had said she wasn't a naïve young girl. Even though she'd had little experience, that was true, in a way. She was twenty-seven years old, a grown woman, a professional with a responsible job, a brilliant career ahead of her. Why shouldn't she take her pleasure where she found it? Why should sex be any different for a woman than it was for a man? No one else thought so these days. What was she saving it for?

But still she couldn't ignore the small voice deep within her that warned her she would be making a terrible mistake to get seriously involved with a man like Nick, with no guarantees, no commitment of any kind. He could so easily break her heart.

By the time she got out of the cold tub, dried off and put on her robe and slippers, it was quarter to ten. Fifteen minutes before he called again, and she was no closer to a solution than she'd been three hours ago.

She went into the living-room, sat down and stared at the telephone, as though she might find an answer to her dilemma there. When its shrill ring broke into the utter stillness of the room at ten o'clock on the dot, it startled her so that she leapt off her chair. With no idea what to say to him, she ran to answer it.

She stopped for a moment to catch her breath, then lifted the receiver. 'Hello,' she said.

'It's Nick,' came his voice. 'Have you made up your mind?'

'Yes,' she said. 'I'll be there tomorrow night.'

She listened to him through a fog as he told her which flight to catch and that he'd be there to pick her up, her head whirling crazily, wondering what on earth had possessed her to blurt it out like that. But it was too late to change her mind now. Then she realised he was still speaking to her.

'I'm really looking forward to seeing you, Regan,' he said in a low, intimate voice.

A great sensation of warmth flooded through her. This was what she wanted. She'd made her decision and she wouldn't look back.

CHAPTER EIGHT

THE dining-room of the lodge at Carmel was located in a separate building, perched high above the roaring surf of the Pacific Ocean at the edge of a rocky promontory. As Regan finished her perfectly cooked steak, she could hardly take her eyes off the man sitting across from her. He was speaking to her, telling her about his trial, but she wasn't really listening to his words.

From the moment she'd really made up her mind to go, all trace of nervousness had miraculously vanished. All during the trip down, meeting Nick at the airport, the drive to Carmel, she had felt as though she was being borne along on a wave of pure bliss.

She hadn't had one moment's regret, not even at the lodge, when he had set her suitcase on the rack next to his in the one bedroom. It helped, too, that he hadn't rushed her. Although the light in his eyes when he first saw her at the air terminal was unmistakable, he'd only put an arm loosely around her shoulders and hugged her to him as they made their way out to the car park, chatting easily, asking about her trip.

It was almost eight o'clock when they arrived at the lodge, and she'd only had time for a quick shower before dinner. Nick had left her alone in the bedroom then, as though in deference to the shyness he must have known she'd be feeling, and, after she'd bathed and changed, they'd walked directly to the restaurant in the gathering dusk.

Sitting across from him now in the elegant restaurant, wearing the pale yellow dress he liked, with the delicious food, the view of the ocean, the candlelight, the wine, it was a romantic experience beyond her wildest dreams. As she watched him, every movement of his hands as he ate or drank, every expression on the lean, expressive face, filled her to overflowing with love and desire.

Although they chatted easily through dinner, mainly about Nick's trial, there was an unmistakable undercurrent of electric tension crackling between them. Regan knew he felt it as powerfully as she did. Neither of them touched on a personal subject, however, until Nick drained the last of his coffee, reached out across the table to take her hand in his and gazed directly into her eyes.

'Are you ready to go?' he asked in a low voice.

She nodded wordlessly, her heart in her mouth, choking with emotion. He pushed his chair back and rose to his feet. Regan got up to join him, and as they walked towards the entrance she could feel his hands on her waist, holding her lightly, guiding her ahead of him.

'How about a short walk to work off some of the food?' he said when they were outside.

'Yes,' she replied. 'I'd like that.'

It was a bright balmy evening, the sky dotted with twinkling stars, a crescent moon hanging low over the phosphorescent surf, and a sharp, salty tang in the air. Although it was dark out by now, the whole area surrounding the lodge was well illuminated by tall light standards.

As they made their way up the steep path to the crest of the hill, his arm tightened around her waist. It was heavy going for Regan in her high-heeled sandals, and she leaned against him, grateful for the support of his tall strength.

There was a small clearing at the top where the path widened, and when they reached it Regan's heel almost buckled under her, twisting her ankle slightly, and she stopped to regain her balance.

'I'm afraid these shoes aren't designed for walking,' she remarked with a little laugh.

'Let's stop for a minute,' he suggested. 'Then, if you like, I can carry you back to the lodge.'

There was a railing at the edge of the clearing, and when they reached it, Regan put her hands on the metal bar and gazed out at the vast ocean, the rocky coast below barely visible in the dark night. Nick was standing behind her, his hands resting lightly on her shoulders. It was a magical moment of perfect contentment, which was only heightened by her anticipation of what lay ahead.

His hands tightened on her, and he leaned down, putting his face against hers. Regan closed her eyes, drinking in his nearness, the scent of him, the rasp of his rough cheek. Then she felt his warm breath in her ear, heard the low sound of his voice.

'I'm so glad you decided to come, Regan,' he murmured. 'I was afraid I'd ruined everything by pushing too hard that night at my place.'

'Oh, no,' she said dreamily. She twisted her head around so that she could look up at him. 'It was probably my fault. I guess I just got cold feet at the last minute.'

'How about now? Any last-minute doubts or reservations?'

She shook her head. 'No. None at all.'

His mouth came down on hers then in a long tender kiss that blotted out all thinking. One hand came around to rest at the base of her throat, and the other slid to the front of her waist. Regan's skin tingled at his touch, her knees felt weak, and she was having trouble breathing.

The hand at her throat moved downward to move lingeringly over her heaving breast in a slow, seductive motion, then slipped under the low bodice to stroke the bare skin beneath it. When he tore his mouth from hers at last, she could hear his own rasping breath, feel the heavy pounding of his heart.

'Shall we go?' he asked in a low, harsh voice.

She didn't trust herself to speak, and could only mutely nod her assent. He turned her around gently to face him. Smiling down at her, he put a hand on her cheek and gave her one last lingering kiss. Then they started walking together towards the lodge, one strong arm still holding her closely to his side.

He didn't release her until they were at their room. He reached into his pocket for the key and unlocked the door. When they were inside, he closed it behind him, and, before turning on a light or uttering a word, he drew her into his arms.

Regan fell against him with a sigh. His mouth came down on hers in a long kiss that grew steadily more urgent, more demanding. They stood there locked together, for a long time, until, finally, he lifted his head and gazed down at her. In the dim glow coming in through the window from the light standards outside, she could see the grey eyes glittering.

'Turn around,' he said softly, propelling her with his hands.

When her back was towards him, she felt his hands at the top fastening of her dress, the zipper being pulled down, the material sliding over her shoulders. He pressed himself up against her, and his hands moved around to unhook the front clasp of her filmy bra.

Then she felt his long fingers pulling aside the material, and those large warm hands covered her bare breasts. She leaned back against him as he moved from one aroused peak to the other, stroking, squeezing gently, moulding the soft firmness.

One hand moved down over her stomach until it reached her thighs, and with a little cry, she turned around. As though possessed by a demon, she tore at the buttons of his shirt, longing to see, to feel, the bare flesh beneath it. When he had shrugged out of the shirt, dropping it to the floor at their feet, he reached out for her again, holding her so that the throbbing tips of her breasts just touched the hard muscled expanse of his bare chest.

Then, in one swift movement, he picked her up in his arms. She clung to him, her head nestled against his shoulder, her eyes closed, as he carried her, until after a few moments she felt herself being gently lowered on to the wide bed.

She opened her eyes to see him standing over her, gazing down at her, and even in the dim room she could make out the tender expression on his face, the firm set to his jaw, the half-closed eyes, and hear his laboured breathing.

'You're so beautiful,' he said in a deep voice that shook with emotion.

Watching him, she thought she had never seen such a breathtaking sight, the tall man, his chest bare, his dark trousers hanging low on his lean hips, and looking at *her*, Regan McIntyre, with the light of desire gleaming in his grey eyes. He reached down to remove the dress, the scraps of lacy underwear, then raised up again and unbuckled his belt.

He sat down beside her and ran his hands over her body, starting at her shoulders, lingering at her breasts, then down to her abdomen, her hips, her thighs. His mouth followed, and, as she felt him take one nipple into his mouth, then the other, she uttered a hoarse cry and reached out for him.

He lay down next to her and took her in his arms, then shifted so that he hovered over her, gazing down at her, his chest heaving. Slowly he lowered himself to cover her body with his.

When Regan awoke some time later, she was still in his arms, facing away from him. She could hear his steady breathing, feel the beat of his heart against her bare back. It was still night, but she had no idea what time it was.

Cautiously she disentangled herself from his long arms and shifted around to face him. He made a low sound somewhere between a grunt and a snort and rolled away from her on to his back, then lay there quite still with one arm flung over his head.

Watching him as he slept, she couldn't resist. Slowly she reached out and touched his forehead, then ran one finger lightly down over that fine patrician nose.

His eyes flicked open and a hand shot out to grasp her by the wrist. He smiled lazily at her, his hair tousled, his eyelids still half-closed.

She returned his smile. 'I've wanted to do that since the first day we met,' she said softly.

He laughed. 'What? Measure my nose? Is there something wrong with it?'

'No. I love your nose. It's perfect.' It was on the tip of her tongue to tell him she loved him, too, but stopped herself just in time. That had to come from him first.

He raised his other hand and placed it on her breast, tracing its contours lightly in slow circles. Regan flushed at the frankly sensual gesture, but the sensations he was arousing in her far outweighed her habitual modesty.

'You have a few physical attributes of your own I've grown quite fond of,' he murmured lazily. 'Come here.'

He held his arms out, and she sank down beside him.

The next morning, after a late leisurely breakfast, they decided to take a drive north on the cliff road that wound along the ocean from Carmel to the peninsula south of San Francisco.

Although it was pleasantly warm when they set out, as the sun rose higher in the blue cloudless sky it became so hot that when Nick stopped for petrol at

Santa Cruz Regan shed the jacket to her white sun-
dress while Nick got out to open all the car windows.

'I hate air-conditioning,' he said when they were on
their way again. 'Do you mind the breeze?'

'No, I love it.' She'd tied a silk scarf around her
head and enjoyed the rush of air on her face.

She would have loved anything in the world at that
point, just so long as she was with him. Tieless, he'd
also taken off his jacket at the petrol station and rolled
up the sleeves of his white shirt to reveal tanned,
muscled forearms covered with smooth dark hair.

She grew misty just gazing at the fine profile, the
wonderful nose, the mouth that had kissed her so
passionately, the strong large hands that had moulded
every inch of her body, the long legs that had inter-
twined with hers during the night.

As she watched him, his gaze suddenly flicked
sideways. Their eyes met, and his white teeth flashed
in a broad appreciative smile.

'You look very fetching in that white outfit,' he
commented. 'Very sexy. What do you call it?'

She glanced down at the neckline. 'It's a halter.'

'Mmm,' he murmured. 'And do I hold the reins to
it?'

She almost blurted out that the hold he had on her
now, after last night, was more powerful than even
he could imagine, but his tone was so light and ban-
tering that she didn't want to spoil the mood by getting
too serious.

'Oh, no,' she replied with a laugh. 'No one does
that.'

'Ah, independent little thing, aren't you?'

'Well, I've had to be, haven't I?'

'I almost forgot,' he said with a knowing nod. 'My liberated woman.'

Regan frowned and turned her eyes straight ahead. Although she knew he was only teasing her and was well aware of how she disliked that term, it still annoyed her. It was almost as though by harping on her 'liberation' he was excusing himself from all responsibility for her.

Then she felt his hand on her knee, squeezing it tight. 'Hey, don't be mad,' he said. 'It's a compliment. I admire your spirit, your independence.'

She gave him a grudging smile. She knew he meant it that way, but each time he mentioned it she was reminded of his determination, stated so firmly right from the beginning, that he would never make a commitment to a career woman. And that meant he saw no future in a relationship with her. What was she supposed to do? Give up her profession, the position she'd worked so hard to get? She would never dream of doing that, not even for him.

They had come to the outskirts of Palo Alto, and soon came to the Stanford University campus, its curving paths and broad green lawns almost deserted now in the summer months.

'That's my old Alma Mater,' Regan remarked casually.

He gave her a startled look. 'Really?' He slowed the car suddenly and made a sharp right into the entrance. 'Then we'd better take a tour of the place.' He glanced at her again as the car crept along. 'How did you manage that? It's a fine institution, probably the best on the West Coast, but also one of the most expensive.'

'Oh, I worked part-time, as well as nights and summers, all through school. That's why it took me five years to finish instead of the usual three. I was lucky enough to win a few scholarships, too.'

He drove slowly around the curving paved road until they came to an isolated spot under the shade of a gigantic old live oak tree. Then he switched off the engine and turned to her.

'I had no idea you were a Stanford graduate. I'm impressed.'

'It's on my résumé,' she commented drily.

He chuckled. 'OK, I'm guilty. You've caught me. At the time it wasn't your credentials I was interested in.'

She eyed him suspiciously. 'What does that mean?'

He shrugged. 'It means that I had other plans for us the moment I laid eyes on you.'

'I can't believe this!' she exclaimed. 'Then what was all that rigmarole about not wanting to work with a woman?'

'I already explained that. Didn't I jump at the chance to move you from my case the minute Jim suggested it?'

She didn't know whether to be insulted or flattered. But by now he'd reached out for her and was pulling her towards him. She turned to face him, and her annoyance evaporated when she saw the familiar gleam in the grey eyes. As his arms came around her, she buried her head in his chest, almost purring with contentment.

'You're a remarkable girl, Regan McIntyre,' he murmured against her cheek. He slid the kerchief back and began to smooth her hair back from her forehead.

'All that hard work and sacrifice to get ahead. And you did it all by yourself.'

'Oh, yes, I'm Wonder Woman.' She raised her head and looked up at him. 'Liberated, too,' she said tartly.

His hand slid down from her hair over her face, then moved lower to travel over her breasts in long lazy strokes, his fingers brushing over the bare skin above the low neckline of her dress. As Regan felt the heat building up inside her, she closed her eyes and made a low sound of pleasure deep in her throat.

'A passionate one, too,' he whispered. His hand slipped inside the bodice. 'I like this halter business of yours,' he murmured as he clutched her bare breast, moulding its soft fullness.

When his open mouth came down to claim hers, she was lost once again under his magic spell. After several long moments, he pulled away and gazed at her. He seemed dazed, his breath rasping, his face suffused with desire, struggling for control.

'You're a witch,' he muttered, withdrawing his hand slowly and lingeringly from inside her dress. 'This isn't exactly the right place for what I have in mind.' He shook his head and frowned. 'I don't know, Regan. You do things to me that no other woman ever has before. I——'

He broke off abruptly, as though afraid he'd already said too much, then turned from her and started the engine again. As they drove off, Regan lay her head back on the seat and closed her eyes, trying to still her own erratic heartbeat. At that moment, she could have sworn he loved her, that he'd even been about to say it. But why didn't he?

* * *

That night a typical summer fog rolled in off the ocean, blanketing the entire area in a fine white mist. After dinner, they hurried back to the lodge through the damp chill air, which was so penetrating that even when they were inside the small sitting-room Regan was still shivering, hugging her arms around her.

'I'm freezing,' she said, making towards the bedroom. 'Think I'll get a sweater and dry off my hair.'

'OK,' Nick said. 'I'll make a fire.'

By the time Regan came back, there was a cheery blaze burning in the stone fireplace. Nick was sitting on the rug in front of it, his back against the couch, his long legs stretched out before him, his arms crossed over his chest.

As she gazed at him, the long lean body, the fire-light flickering over the strong features, a pensive, rather withdrawn expression on his face, her knees grew weak at the great surge of helpless love for him that swept over her.

He'd been rather quiet since their drive up the coast that afternoon, and, although he was always good company, he'd seemed abstracted during dinner. She'd tried asking him about his case, but, when he barely answered her questions on a subject that normally elicited great enthusiasm, she could tell he had his mind on something else.

Something had changed between them, and it had to have happened that afternoon. She searched her mind. At Stanford he'd mentioned her 'liberation' once again. Why did he keep harping on that? Although he claimed to admire her spirit and independence, the obstacles she'd overcome, the sacrifices she'd made to get the best education, it almost seemed at times that he resented it.

She skirted around him and stood in front of the fire, her back towards it, looking down at him. He gazed up at her and gave her a lazy smile, then held out a hand.

'Come and sit with me,' he said.

She took his hand, and he pulled her down in front of him, raising his knees to make room for her between his legs. When she settled back against him, he put his arms around her, crossing them loosely in front of her.

'Warm enough now?' he murmured next to her ear.

'Mm,' she purred. 'Toasty.'

They sat there in a contented silence, his chin resting on the top of her head, rubbing his hands idly up and down her arms. Through the thin sweater his touch was electric, and she wished it could always be like this, just the two of them, so close, with none of the harsh realities of life to spoil it.

Did he love her, just a little? She wished she could get inside his head. She wanted to know everything about him, what had made him the kind of man he was.

After a while she twisted around to face him. 'Tell me about your family, Nick,' she said.

'What do you want to know?'

'Well, you said you had two brothers and three sisters. What do they do?'

He smiled and kissed her on the nose. 'Well, let's see. Mike is a doctor, a paediatrician, and Greg is an electronics engineer.'

'And?' she prompted when he didn't continue.

'And what?' he asked in a puzzled tone.

She laughed. 'That's only two out of five. What about your sisters?'

'Well, Sue is married to a——'

She put a finger on his mouth. 'I don't want to know what their husbands do. You and your brothers are educated, professional men. What do your sisters do?'

He frowned. 'They stay home and take care of their homes, their husbands and their children.'

Regan froze. 'I see,' she said in a tight voice. 'Just like your mother.'

He shrugged. 'They're happy.'

'Are you sure?'

He eyed her coolly for several long seconds without saying anything. Regan could sense the growing tension building up between them, feel him almost literally withdraw from her. Why had she even brought the subject up? It was none of her business. Thousands of women were happy staying at home taking care of families. She tried to think of a more neutral subject, but, before she could come up with anything suitable, he had shifted his weight behind her and was rising to his feet.

He went over to the fire, picked up the poker and jabbed at it, raising a shower of sparks. He replaced the poker, grabbed the small broom and swept the cinders off the hearth, all in slow, deliberate motions. Finally, he turned around, his jaw set, his eyes narrowed at her.

'I don't understand why you career women always have to put down women who choose to stay home and take care of their families,' he said in his most persuasive courtroom voice. 'You act as though it's some kind of imprisonment, or a punishment inflicted on them by chauvinistic men. Has it ever occurred to you that raising the next generation just might be as important as practising law or medicine? My sisters chose their lives, just as my mother chose hers.'

'You're right, of course,' Regan said quickly. 'I didn't mean it that way. I'm sorry. I wasn't trying to judge them, or women like them, but I do get rather tired of people implying that's what all women should do.'

'Weren't you implying that all women should have careers?' he shot back immediately.

'Not really. I just don't see that family and career are necessarily incompatible.'

'Well, I think they are,' he said stiffly.

Regan shifted uneasily and stared into the fire. She hadn't meant her casual remark that way, and he knew it. She gazed up at him. He was stony-faced and brooding, his eyes fixed on the floor. Why was he taking it all so personally? It wasn't like him.

Fear clutched at her heart. She was not going to lose him over one thoughtless comment on a subject that didn't even interest her at the moment. Quickly she jumped to her feet and crossed over to him. Without a word, she put her arms around his waist and buried her head in his chest.

He stood there perfectly rigid for some time, but gradually she felt his body thaw against her. He put his arms around her and his hands started moving up and down her back in slow rhythmic strokes. After a while, she raised her head to look up at him.

'Friends?' she asked with a smile.

He gazed down at her, his face expressionless, for several long seconds, then, finally, his mouth creased in a smile and he hugged her closer to him, his face buried in her hair, his mouth at her ear.

'What am I going to do with you, Regan?' he murmured. 'You can be so maddening, yet I can't seem to get enough of you.' He raised his head and shook it in genuine bewilderment. 'What in the world am I going to do with you?' he repeated.

She gave him a brilliant smile as waves of relief flooded through her. 'I have a suggestion,' she said mischievously.

He raised an eyebrow. 'Oh? Will I like it?'

She nodded. 'I think so.'

The rest of the weekend passed so swiftly that on Monday afternoon, as she packed her one bag, Regan could hardly believe it was actually time to go home. They planned to leave for the city at five o'clock to catch her seven-thirty flight.

Nick had gone to the office to pay the bill, and it was the first time all weekend she'd been alone. Already she missed him. She'd become so accustomed to his constant presence at her side that she felt like half a person without him.

If she'd thought she was falling in love with him before, these three wonderful days alone with him had pushed her completely over the edge. She'd known he was a passionate man, but never dreamed he was capable of such tenderness and consideration for her needs.

She had just finished putting the last article of clothing in her suitcase when she heard him come in.

She looked up and smiled at him when he appeared in the doorway. He was dressed in a dark business suit, crisp white shirt and tie, and the expression on his face was serious and abstracted. A sharp jab of panic clutched at Regan's heart. He was already leaving her.

'Are you almost ready?' he said, glancing at his watch. 'The freeway traffic will be heavy this time of day.'

'Yes,' she replied, snapping the bag shut.

He came over and picked it up. 'We're all set, then.'

Regan followed him out to his rental car. She would have liked one last lingering look at the two small rooms where she'd been so happy, but, since he was obviously anxious to get going, she hurried after him and got inside the car while he stowed her bag in the back.

The drive to the airport in San Francisco was largely a silent one. The traffic was indeed heavy, but Regan knew there was more than that to his concentrated frown. He was obviously putting a distance between them, his mind most likely on his trial, which was to resume tomorrow.

Even that didn't explain everything, however, and, the closer they came to the city, the stronger Regan's anxiety grew. Something else was on his mind, had been ever since the drive to Palo Alto on Saturday and the brief, heated discussion they'd had that evening. After that, something had changed. Although his lovemaking had remained passionate, she could sense him receding from her in other ways, pushing her away, almost as though he had been protecting himself, hiding his feelings from her.

Several times it had been on the tip of her tongue to ask him about it. Perhaps he'd been disappointed with her, her inexperience, her shyness. Yet she had responded to him with reckless abandon, meeting him every step of the way. His lovemaking had ranged from the tenderest restraint to the verge of violence, but she hadn't once hesitated or held back anything.

At the airport, he parked the car and they went into the terminal. They'd just made it in time, and her flight was announced as soon as she'd checked her bag. He seemed almost relieved as he walked with her to the gate, and it dawned on her for the first time that he hadn't touched her once that entire day.

'Well, have a safe trip,' he said just outside the gate.

She moved closer to him, hoping he would take her in his arms, kiss her goodbye, say something. Anything! But his hands remained stuck in his trouser pockets. She tried to catch his eye, but his gaze had already darted past her towards the crowds streaming by behind her on their way to the plane.

'Thanks for the lovely weekend, Nick,' she said at last in desperation. 'I had a wonderful time.'

He gave her a brief nod. 'Thank you for coming,' he replied politely. 'It was great.'

She could hardly believe her ears. He might have been thanking her for a job well done! She couldn't help it. She couldn't leave like this. She had to know. If she didn't speak now she might not get another chance. She looked up at him, directly into his eyes, forcing him to meet her steady gaze.

'Nick, is something wrong?' she asked quietly.

Something flickered in his eyes, a look of such yearning it took her breath away. Suddenly he gripped her by the shoulders so hard she was almost lifted off her feet, and his mouth came down to grind against hers in a searing kiss that seemed almost desperate in its intensity. Then, just as suddenly, he released her.

'You'd better go now,' he said. 'You'll miss your flight.'

'Yes. Well, goodbye for now, then.'

'Goodbye,' he said, and the relief in his voice was unmistakable.

Regan joined the last stragglers and walked slowly down the ramp towards the van that would take them out to the plane. Just before she stepped inside, she turned around for one last look. But he was already gone.

By the time she arrived at her apartment that night, she was sunk in a profound depression. All during the plane trip and the taxi ride from the airport, away from his powerful presence, she went over every moment of the time she had spent with him, looking for clues as to the meaning of that last punishing kiss. It had seemed ominously like a last farewell.

He'd never once said he loved her, but she hadn't really expected that. Not yet. What she had hoped for, however, even thought she had a reasonable right to expect, was some discussion about their future, some sign that he cared about her after she'd given herself to him so unreservedly. But he hadn't even come close.

Yet there had been moments that she couldn't quite forget. Even though she was afraid she might be grasping at straws, she still felt that he had come close to some kind of declaration that day on the Stanford campus. And, during their lovemaking, he had treated her with a tenderness and sensitivity that couldn't have been faked just for the sake of an easy conquest. There were times when she'd caught him looking at her in a certain way that exactly mirrored her own feelings, times when she could have sworn he did love her.

Then gradually, his ardour had cooled. What had happened to change him? The man was an enigma, one moment full of admiration for her accomplishments, the next holding up his mother and sisters as shining ideals of glorious womanhood. No wonder she was so confused. He obviously wasn't as sure of his own convictions as he made out.

She wandered gloomily around her apartment, unpacking, picking at the remains of a ham she had left in the fridge on Friday, leafing through the accumulated mail and newspapers. At eleven o'clock, she took a bath and got into bed. As she lay there, staring blankly up at the ceiling, she had to face the thing she'd feared the most: that she must have only been another conquest to him.

By now, however, she was in so deep over her head that she didn't even care. If it was that or nothing, she'd just have to accept it. All she knew was that she wanted him on any terms.

'What in the world is wrong with you, Regan?'

Regan looked up from her desk to see Jim Courtney standing at the door to her office. His usual kindly round face was creased in a scowl, and he was holding out a thick document as though it were a ticking bomb. She recognised it as the final draft of the contract she had put on his desk that morning, the last step in the bank merger.

'Nothing's wrong,' she replied. 'Why?'

'This contract of yours,' he pronounced testily, tossing it down on her desk. 'You've left out two of the most critical clauses. If our clients were to sign this the way it is now, they'd be bankrupt in six months.'

'Sorry,' she mumbled. Flushing deeply, she picked up the contract and began to leaf through it. It was a mere jumble of meaningless words to her, but she had to put on some kind of front to convince him that she was at least marginally interested in it.

He turned on his heel and walked out. Regan gazed dully after him. How could she tell him that her heart was broken? She simply had to get hold of herself. The last thing she wanted was to lose her job. It was all she had, now.

It had been three weeks since she'd returned from the weekend at Carmel, three bleak dreary weeks of unremitting sunshine, when hardly a moment had passed that she didn't think of him. She'd sat by her telephone each night, refusing every invitation, so that even Don had ceased asking her to do things with him.

She didn't even have coffee with the other lawyers any more. Not only did any company at all grate on her nerves, but she was literally terrified she might run into Nick if she set foot on the floor below. As far as she knew he hadn't been back, but if she should see him she simply didn't trust herself not to fall apart entirely, create a scene, burst into tears.

It was time to take action, anything to snap her out of this dreadful gloomy lethargy.

That afternoon Regan worked hard to rectify her errors in the merger contract, and had it on Jim's desk by five o'clock. She already felt better. He was right. What she needed to snap out of her passive gloom was to take some positive action.

On that basis, it was also time to put herself out of her misery as far as Nick was concerned, to find out one way or another just what was going on, what his intentions were. She had nothing at all to lose. It was hell not knowing, still hoping. She was tired of telling herself he was too busy to call her. No matter how swamped he was, he could find time for a five-minute phone call.

As soon as she got home that evening, she marched straight to the telephone and dialled the number of his hotel in San Francisco before she could change her mind. It was six o'clock. Court sessions usually ended at four-thirty. He should be in his room by now getting ready for dinner.

When his voice came on the line, she almost lost her nerve and was strongly tempted to slam the receiver down. It took every ounce of will power she possessed to speak to him.

'Hello, Nick. It's Regan.'

During the short silence that followed, she could have sworn she heard a quick intake of breath, but when he spoke, his voice was bland and guarded. 'How are you, Regan?' he asked quietly.

'Quite well, thanks.' She took a deep breath. 'I've been thinking about inviting myself down for another weekend. I could make it this Friday night if you're free.'

'Gosh, I'm sorry, Regan, but a group of us are going down to Carmel to discuss settlement. One of the defendant lawyers has a house there, and we thought we'd make more headway in an informal setting.' He hesitated. 'I *am* sorry. Maybe some other time.'

Well, now she knew. She stood there, rigid, filled with a sickening sense of disappointment, fighting a losing battle with the tears she couldn't hold back. By now she didn't even care.

'No, Nick,' she said, her voice catching on a sob. 'There won't be another time. That's OK,' she rushed on hurriedly. 'You never made me any promises. You're home free, no strings, no messy scene. But you could have told me.'

'Regan, don't,' he broke in. 'It's not what you think. Believe me, it's better this way. You don't under-stand——'

'Oh?' Her voice rose on a note of hysteria, and she was sobbing openly by now. 'I think I understand quite well. I was just another easy conquest to you, wasn't I?'

She hated this display of weakness, but by now was totally unable to stop herself, and, before he could get in a word, she rushed on. 'I don't even blame you for that. I knew what I was getting into, the risk I was taking. But what I'll never forgive is that you didn't have the guts to be honest with me about it,

that you led me to believe you cared something about
me, then just dumped me when it suited you.'

'Regan——' he began.

'Oh, go to hell!' she cried, and slammed the receiver down.

CHAPTER NINE

FROM that night on, Regan began to feel better. It had done her self-esteem a world of good to have been the one to break it off with Nick. Although there was still a gaping hole in her heart that she was afraid might never be filled again, she was coping. The important thing was to get her life in order again. Nick had burst in and out of it like a tornado, and, the sooner she started picking up the pieces, the sooner she'd get over him.

The very next night, old faithful Don came doggedly to her door and asked her to have dinner with him. She'd put him off so many times in the past month that when she promptly agreed he only stood there gawping at her.

'You will?' he asked.

She had to smile. He was too comical for words, with his sandy hair standing up on end, his shabby clothes, his frank, open face that could hide nothing. He obviously cared for her. Why else would he keep coming when she'd done everything under the sun to discourage him? In fact, she'd treated him rather badly. Once again, she wished she could fall in love with him.

'Don, I'm really sorry I've been such a pig lately,' she said on a more serious note.

'Oh, that's OK,' he said with a blithe wave of his hand. 'I'm so used to getting dumped on at the hospital that I wouldn't know how to act if anyone was nice to me.'

Her performance on the job also continued to improve, and she was soon working up to her old standards, without any more careless mistakes. Although at first it took real courage to venture down to Nick's floor, where the library and coffee-room were located, after a few weeks she was even able to pass by his office without trembling or averting her eyes.

He was never in there anyway. Apparently his trial was still running, and, as Regan's confidence slowly returned, she began to nurse the hope that, by the time he did come back, she would be well over him for good.

It was late August by now, and autumn was just around the corner, with heavy morning fogs, clear crisp days and cooler nights. It was Regan's favourite time of year. Her work was going well, and she had even been able to work up an interest in Jim's bank merger.

One Monday morning when she arrived in her office, there was a note on top of her desk from Jim Courtney, telling her he would be out of town for a few days and asking her to finish up the last item of research on the bank merger contract so that it could be signed when he got back.

She picked up a yellow legal pad and a sharp pencil and made her way down the stairs to the library. It should only take half an hour, then the word processing centre could insert it in the draft contract and it would be ready to give to Jim for final approval.

As she started to turn into the library, her mind was so engrossed in the exact text she needed to look up that she didn't notice the tall man walking towards her until she almost collided with him. She glanced up to apologise, and found herself gazing into the stony grey eyes of Nick Wainwright.

It was a shock, but she covered it quickly. She made her face a mask, nodded calmly at him and even managed to force out a thin smile.

'Hello, Nick,' she said. 'Back from the wars, I see.'

Before he could answer her, she'd breezed on past him, her head high, her arms stiff at her sides, clutching her pencil so hard it actually snapped in half by the time she reached an unoccupied desk over by the contracts section. She found the book she needed, sat down and flipped it open.

After a few moments of staring down blankly at the page in front of her, the words swimming before her eyes, she finally dared a glance in the direction of the door. There was no one there.

By a miracle of concentrated effort, she finally got her bit of research completed, drafted the clause to be inserted in the contract, and dropped it off at the word processing centre. Then she went back upstairs to her own office and sat down at her desk.

Although she was still shaken from the encounter with Nick, her reaction to him had been rather different from what she'd expected. Somehow, at the sight of him, all the bitterness she'd been nursing these past several weeks had simply vanished into thin air. All she felt now was a void, a kind of dead emptiness.

How could she be angry at him? By his code of ethics, he hadn't behaved badly towards her. He'd made it absolutely clear right from the beginning what to expect from him, and he hadn't pushed her into anything she hadn't wanted badly herself.

He was only a man, after all, and, although he no longer had the power to awe or intimidate her, she could still look back on her experience with him and remember the joys. There was no point in dwelling on the sorrows.

Buoyed up by her success in facing him without falling to pieces, she decided to go back downstairs to the coffee-room for a short break. She had just risen to her feet when the door to her office opened, and Nick stepped inside.

He stood there for a moment staring fixedly at her, scowling darkly, then closed the door behind him and walked slowly towards her. He sat down on the chair across from her, crossed one long leg over the other, and gave her a narrow-eyed penetrating look.

'I want to talk to you,' he said finally.

She cupped her chin in her hand and gave him a bright, alert look. 'Yes?' she said.

He hesitated a moment, then said, 'How have you been?'

'Fine.'

'You look a little pale.'

'Oh?'

He uncrossed his legs and leaned forward, his arms resting on his knees. 'Listen, Regan,' he said in a low voice. 'I feel terrible about the way things have turned out between us.'

He felt terrible! 'Why is that?' she asked curtly. She was determined not to help him.

The frown deepened. 'You're not making this any easier for me,' he growled.

Regan glanced at her watch. 'Could you speed it up a little, Nick? I have to do a couple of things that are fairly urgent.'

A deep red flush spread over his face. 'All right,' he muttered gruffly. 'I guess I deserved that. I just wanted to tell you I'm sorry.'

'Well, it's a little late for that, isn't it, Nick?'

He flushed again. 'Listen, I've been swamped down there with my trial. I'd still be there if we hadn't settled. In fact, I just got back in town yesterday.' He hesitated for a moment, then cleared his throat and went on. 'Now that I'm back for good, I was thinking that I'd like to try to pick up where we left off.'

For the first time a flicker of hope flared up in Regan's heart. She eyed him carefully. Even after all that had happened, he still could wield immense power over her if she let him. Her love for him had been too strong to be forgotten so soon.

But, no matter what he said now, he'd proved in every way possible that he didn't care about her, that she was only an annoyance he wanted to get rid of as painlessly—to him!—as possible. She couldn't back down now. It had cost her too much to give him up once. If she weakened now, she might not be able to do it again.

She shook her head slowly, sadly. 'I'm afraid that's not on the cards, Nick,' she said. 'It's too late.'

He got up out of his chair, braced his hands on top of the desk, and leaned towards her. 'Listen, as swamped as I was with that trial, I thought about calling you several times. In fact, I did call you. Twice. But you didn't answer.'

'Well, we really didn't have anything more to say to each other, did we?' She started walking towards the door. 'Now I really have to get on. It's important.'

He straightened up and folded his arms across his chest, his steely eyes fixed on her every step of the way. As she passed by him, not six inches away, a hand shot out and closed around her arm in an iron grip.

'You're going to walk out?' he barked angrily. 'Just like that?'

She raised her chin and looked him straight in the eye. 'Yes, Nick. Just like that. Now let me go.'

'I'm willing to try again to explain why I acted the way I did, Regan,' he said in a warning tone. 'But I'm not going to beg.'

'No one asked you to,' she snapped.

She shook her arm free and hurried on out into the corridor without a backward glance. She slipped quickly into Jim's office, closed the door behind her, and leaned back against it, her eyes shut tight. The emotions she'd thought were gone had all been aroused again by the painful encounter. Warring within her were love, hatred, anger, and regret, and she couldn't begin to sort them out.

From then on everything started to go downhill for Regan. In the office she seemed to come across Nick at every turn, in the library, the coffee-room, the lift, on the stairs, so that she actually dreaded to go to work in the morning. She began to develop throbbing headaches that would suddenly come upon her out of nowhere. Her normally healthy appetite vanished, and her stomach turned over in actual physical revulsion at the mere thought of food.

She was also having trouble sleeping and would lie in bed each night tossing and turning, trying to keep the haunting images out of her mind. She wasn't really sick, at least not enough to stay home from work, but she was far from well.

Eventually, of course, being a doctor, Don noticed it. They had formed the habit of eating dinner together whenever he had a night off from the hospital, and one evening as they sat in her apartment eating a Chinese take-away, she looked up to see him staring at her, a pensive expression on his face.

'What's wrong?' she asked.

He shrugged. 'I was just wondering what's happened to your old voracious appetite. I remember when you would gobble down hot Mongolian beef as though there was no tomorrow. Now you barely touch it. You don't look so hot, either.'

She laughed. 'Thanks a lot. That does a lot for my poor battered ego.'

Don nodded owlishly. 'That's what I mean. It always seemed to me that you had a pretty healthy ego. But, lately, you act as though you're carrying the weight of the world around on your shoulders. Is the job getting you down? Or is it something more personal?' He hesitated for a moment, then his face grew solemn. 'How are things working out for you in that department?' he asked cautiously. 'I mean, with your boss.'

'Well,' she replied with a shaky smile. 'As a matter of fact, they aren't working out at all.'

'Gosh, I'm sorry, Regan. Do you want to talk about it?'

She shook her head. 'Not really. Let's just say I made a bad mistake. You were right. Remember? You said I could end up sadder but wiser.' Suddenly she felt the hot tears sting behind her eyes. All it took was Don's sympathetic attitude to push her over the edge. She covered her face with her hands. 'Oh, Don,' she blubbered, 'I've been such a fool.'

'Hey,' he said, moving towards her and putting an arm around her heaving shoulders. 'It can't be as bad as all that.' He patted her awkwardly on the back while she sobbed quietly into his shoulder. 'You're a wonderful girl, Regan. You've got it all, brains, looks, guts. Any man would be lucky to get you.'

Finally, she groped in her pocket for a tissue, wiped her eyes and blew her nose. If she was going to have a minor breakdown, it was just as well she'd done it with Don instead of the whole office.

She blinked up at him. 'Well, thanks for the testimonial, anyway,' she said with a loud sniff. 'You're a real friend, Don.'

'Do you feel like telling me what happened now?'

'Oh, it's the same old boring story. I just fell in love with the wrong person. I knew what he was like right from the start, so I have no one to blame but myself.' She sighed deeply and blew her nose again. 'Why is it that women always seem to think they can make a leopard change its spots when it comes to difficult men?'

'Well, all I can say is that the guy's a damn fool,' Don remarked gruffly. 'You're too good for him, that's what it really amounts to.'

'You're right,' she agreed promptly. 'You're absolutely right.'

Don smiled, but he still looked worried. 'Listen, Regan,' he said quietly, 'while I realise that people don't really die of a broken heart, I still don't like the way you're looking. Why don't you come up to the hospital tomorrow and I'll have one of our best internists take a look at you.'

'Oh, Don, I don't think that's necessary.'

'Just to please me,' he insisted.

She couldn't refuse, and to tell the truth she was getting a little tired of dragging around feeling so rotten all the time.

The next afternoon, a very stern, elderly doctor informed Regan that she was ten pounds underweight and had borderline anaemia. He quizzed her about her diet, sleep habits, stress at work, and she tried to answer as honestly as she could without mentioning her personal life.

'It sounds to me, young lady, as though you're suffering from professional burnout.'

'What's that?'

'It means that the pressures in your work situation have mounted up to the point where they've made you physically ill. It's time to seriously consider a change before you develop a full-blown illness. The body can take just so much mental stress before it reacts and starts to break down.'

'I'm sorry, Doctor,' she said with a wry smile, 'but I've worked too hard at my profession to give it up over what's probably a temporary bit of stress. Can't I take vitamins or something?'

He chuckled. 'Well, vitamins can't hurt. But I wasn't suggesting you give up the law, only that there might be something in your present environment that is upsetting you—uncongenial work, friction with co-workers, perhaps a difficult superior.'

Or a disastrous love affair, she added silently. 'All right,' she said aloud, rising to her feet. 'Thank you, Doctor. I'll give it some serious thought.'

He scribbled something on a prescription pad, tore it off and handed it to her. 'In the meantime, try these potent vitamins. They might help get you over the hump.'

She left his office feeling profoundly depressed. Just when she had thought she was getting a firm foothold on her life after the shattering experience with Nick, her health had to go to pieces.

Don was waiting for her in the hall and managed to get away long enough to go with her to the hospital cafeteria for a cup of coffee. When they were sitting down, he raised an eyebrow at her.

'Well? What's the verdict?'

She laughed bitterly. 'He says I'm under too much stress at work. Suggests I make a change.'

He hesitated for a moment. 'What are you going to do?' he asked slowly.

She shrugged. 'I don't know.'

'Maybe you should think about leaving altogether.'

She nodded glumly. 'Maybe I should.'

Late that night, Regan stood at the window of her darkened living-room, gazing blankly out at the starlit sky, in an agony of mind and spirit, wondering what in the world she was going to do.

For the hundredth time that day, she went carefully over her alternatives. If only she weren't so alone! Then it suddenly occurred to her that she really wasn't. She whirled around, switched on a light and ran to the telephone. With shaking fingers, she dialled her father's number. When she heard his familiar voice on the line, she almost sobbed aloud with relief.

After the brief preliminaries, she took a deep breath and went straight to the point. 'Daddy,' she said. 'I have a problem and need to talk it over with you.'

He chuckled deep in his throat. 'Well, honey, that's what fathers are for, aren't they? Come on. Spill it.'

When she tried to actually form the words, all that came out was a strangled sob. She squeezed her eyes shut tight, drew in a deep breath and tried again, but still couldn't make herself say it. He'd be so disappointed in her, especially after all his warnings about dangerous men. At the time she'd laughed it off. If only she'd listened to him then!

Then she heard him speaking in a low voice. 'Maybe we'd better play twenty questions,' he said calmly. 'Are you pregnant?'

She gave a strangled laugh at that. Leave it to her old-fashioned father to consider an unmarried pregnancy the worst thing that could possibly happen to her. He would almost rather have her confess to an actual crime.

'No, Daddy,' she said. 'Don't worry, it's not that.' She went on to tell him the whole thing, the affair with Nick, the way he'd dropped her, her incipient illness and the doctor's advice.

'Well, I'll tell you what to do,' he replied in a loud firm voice. 'It's quite simple. You'll quit your job, come home and let me and your sisters spoil you for a while. Between us we'll figure out what to do.'

After they hung up Regan went to her desk in the living-room and typed out a letter of resignation, then went straight to bed to sleep soundly for the first time in weeks.

The next morning Jim Courtney wasn't in his office when Regan arrived at work. She debated leaving the letter of resignation she'd prepared last night on his desk, but decided it would be better to give it to him in person. She owed him that much for all his kindness to her.

She went next door to her own room. The morning fog had burned off, and a warm August sun was coming in through the window. Down below, the blue waters of Puget Sound sparkled, the mountains glistening in the background. She'd miss all this. She'd worked so hard to get here, and now she'd have to leave it behind.

It was the last thing in the world she wanted to do, but there were other law firms. She needed to get away—from the job, from Seattle, but especially from Nick—if she were to put her life together again.

She went next door again to see if Jim had come back. He was sitting behind his desk, and when she came inside he glanced up.

'Well, Regan?' he said. 'Is something wrong?'

She went to his desk and held out the envelope she was still carrying. 'I wanted to give you this in person.'

Jim raised an eyebrow. 'What is it?'

'My letter of resignation.'

Jim half rose out of his chair, a shocked expression on his face. 'Why?'

She hated to lie to him. He'd been too kind to her. But since she couldn't tell him the complete truth, either, she decided to temporise.

'I haven't been feeling well lately,' she said at last. 'I've seen a doctor, and he advised me to take some time off.' When she saw the look of alarm on his face, she raised a hand. 'It's not serious, nothing life-threatening. I just need a good rest.'

Jim sat back down and gave her a look of genuine concern. 'I'm sorry, Regan,' he said, obviously meaning it. 'Your work here has been superior. We'll hate to lose you.' He eyed her thoughtfully. 'Would you consider taking a leave of absence?'

For a moment, she was tempted. But it would never work out. She couldn't possibly work in the same office with Nick again. At this point it wasn't even safe to work in the same city with him!

She shook her head. 'That's very kind of you, Jim,' she said. 'But right now I have no idea how long it'll be. I think it's best for all concerned if I leave permanently.'

'What will you do?' he asked quietly. 'If you need money, a loan perhaps . . .'

'Thanks, but I've decided to go home, back to Yakima. My father wants me to, and we'll manage until I feel well enough to go back to work.'

He persisted in presenting alternatives to her for the next half-hour, but when she politely but firmly declined each one he came up with, he finally gave it up. They parted on good terms, and he offered to write her a letter of recommendation, which she gratefully accepted. There was no sense in burning bridges.

That very night, she started to pack. Jim had kindly agreed that, since the merger she'd been working on was completed at last, there was no reason for her to give the usual month's notice, especially considering that her health was at issue. There was nothing to keep her in Seattle, and her father had insisted that she come home as soon as possible. Don was on duty at the hospital that night, but she could say goodbye to him the next morning before she left.

She had just finished packing the last suitcase when the front doorbell rang. She glanced at her watch. It was ten o'clock. Maybe Don had been able to get off earlier than he expected.

She went to the door and opened it, then backed off a step when she saw Nick standing there.

'Oh,' she said. 'It's you.'

His face was pinched and white, and there was an expression on it she'd never seen before, almost as though he were in pain. There was real hurt in the grey eyes, and the little lines at the corners were deeply etched.

'Yes,' he said in a tight voice. 'It's me. May I come in?'

'I'm terribly busy right now——' she began.

But he was already inside, closing the door behind him. 'This won't take long,' he said. He stood there for a moment looking down at her, his hands stuck in his trouser pockets, his mouth twisted, his eyes narrowed. 'Jim tells me you've resigned from the firm.'

'Yes,' she replied shortly.

'Why?'

She turned from him. 'I don't see that that's any of your business.'

Before she'd gone a step, he'd reached out with both hands and forced her around to face him. He glared down at her, his eyes blazing. His fingers bit into her shoulders, his chest was heaving, and he was obviously making an effort to control himself. Finally, he relaxed his grip on her and the eyes softened.

'I told you once that I wouldn't beg, Regan,' he said softly. 'But it looks as though I'm going to have to.'

'Nick, I don't want you to beg.' By now she was on the verge of tears. 'I just want you to leave me alone.'

'All I ask is that you listen to me. Half an hour, an hour at the most. Then, if you want me to, I'll go away and never bother you again. Will you do that much for me?'

How could she resist? Besides, she was curious. What did he want from her? Her plans were all made. She'd quit her job, her father was expecting her tomorrow, she was all packed. It wouldn't hurt just to listen to what he had to say.

'All right,' she agreed. 'Come on in.'

He followed her into the living-room, and they sat down at opposite ends of the couch. He sat for some time with his head bowed, his hands laced in front of him, apparently deep in thought. Finally, he turned to her.

'A few weeks ago,' he began quietly, 'I told you that the reason I hadn't called you or made any effort to see you after that weekend in Carmel was because I was under pressure from my trial. That wasn't true.' He shrugged. 'Or only partly true. But there was more to it, a lot more.'

She waited, totally in the dark, but, when he didn't go on, she felt she had to speak. 'That's not exactly news to me,' she said with a bitterness she couldn't disguise. 'For a long time I made excuses like that for you, but in the end even I had to face the fact that if you'd really wanted to see me or talk to me you would have found a way.' She frowned and made an impatient gesture. 'But I still don't see the point of going into all this again.'

'I know I'm explaining it badly.' He hesitated. 'That time we spent in Carmel,' he said slowly, 'it was wonderful.' He smiled for the first time, a sad, rueful smile. 'Damn near perfect.'

'Up to a point,' she said. 'Then something happened to ruin it, didn't it? It doesn't really matter now, but I'd like to know. Was it me? Something I did? Or didn't do?'

'No!' he shot out immediately. 'Absolutely not. You were everything I could have hoped for. It was my fault entirely.' He gazed at her bleakly. 'The truth of the matter is that you terrified me, scared me out of my wits, and all I could think of was to run.'

If he had suddenly turned to stone before her eyes, she couldn't have been more shocked. '*I* terrified *you*?' she exclaimed. She forced out a harsh laugh. 'If that wasn't so ridiculous, it would be funny. How was I any threat to you? I *worshipped* you, Nick!' Her voice broke, and she turned her head away.

'Well, damn it, didn't it ever occur to you that I felt the same way?'

She stared at him, open-mouthed. 'No,' she stated flatly. 'Not in a million years.'

By now he had edged closer to her on the couch. At the slight pressure of his body against hers, an insistent warmth began to steal through her, and, when he reached out to take her hand in his, she didn't have the strength to resist. His bald statement had shocked her into weak immobility. Her head was whirling crazily. All she could do was sit and wait for what came next.

'I realise now that I was already half in love with you even before Carmel,' he said in a low voice. 'All it took was that one wonderful weekend, and I knew I was getting in too deep. I felt I had to get you out of my mind and heart before I fell all the way. But it was already too late.' He gave her a pleading look. 'Regan, I know I've hurt you, but won't you try to look at it from my point of view? On the one hand, you were becoming indispensable to me. I wanted you at any price. But on the other, if I let myself love you, make a commitment, I was afraid we'd end up in the kind of domestic mess I'd sworn I'd never get into. I didn't know which way to turn.'

'Nick,' she said, gazing deeply into his eyes. 'Why are you telling me this now?'

He rose abruptly from the couch and strode across the room. He stood there for a long time, his shoulders slumped forward, his head bent. Finally, he turned around and gave her a stricken look.

'Because,' he ground out harshly, 'in spite of all my grand principles and pet theories about careers and marriage not working, I can't live without you. Once the trial was over, I had a vague idea that we might be able to at least see each other, perhaps even have an affair, with no commitment. Then, today, when Jim told me you'd resigned, I realised I simply couldn't risk letting you walk out of my life.'

With her whole heart, Regan wanted to believe him, and for one moment she was tempted to close her eyes and blindly take the plunge, but she couldn't quite accept his speech at face value. There had to be more to it than he was telling her. Although it sounded as though he really had cared for her, and still did, he seemed to be no closer to making promises than ever.

He wanted her, that much was clear, even claimed he was *half* in love with her. And she wanted him. Oh, how she wanted him! Even now, humbled, pleading, in obvious distress, he still had enormous power to turn her knees to water, set her heart pounding. She still loved him, even more than ever. But could she afford to give her whole heart to a man who was afraid of commitment to a woman with any interest in life besides him?

Then she knew she couldn't do that, couldn't enter into any kind of relationship with him without a complete understanding. She gave him a quick glance. He was obviously waiting for her to speak.

'What actually did happen, Nick, that weekend in Carmel?' she asked quietly.

He ran a hand over his hair and stared pensively down at his feet for a moment, then began speaking again in a low voice. 'Everything was going beautifully until that afternoon when we were at Stanford. Then something just snapped suddenly in my mind.'

He shook his head impatiently. 'I don't know, somehow I really grasped for the first time what courage and character it took for you to get your education, and how much I admired those qualities in you.

'Then that same night, when you asked about my family, that really triggered off the alarm. I think I'd been searching all my life, in every woman I'd known, for an ideal, but never could find her.' He smiled diffidently. 'Perhaps, like most men, I wanted a duplicate of my mother, or at least a woman like her, one who could centre her life on her husband and family without any nonsense about a career. Then you came along, with your spunk and determination, and all my old convictions began to topple.'

He shrugged. 'All I could think of then was to get out, while there was still time. Pretty cowardly, huh?'

She didn't say anything, couldn't think of anything to say.

'Then,' he went on, 'today, when Jim told me you'd resigned, it all came crashing down around me. Never to see you again, never to touch you, kiss you, hold you. As long as you were working in the same office I'd at least see you once in a while, like forbidden fruit. It was torture, but nothing compared to not seeing you at all.' He took a deep breath. 'As a matter of fact, when Jim said you had a health problem, for a moment I thought just maybe you might be pregnant. I knew it was very unlikely, but the timing was about right.'

'Well, I'm not,' she declared firmly.

'I know, but the point is—my immediate, instinctive reaction was a rush of pure joy at the thought of pro-

ducing a child. Our child.' He paused, then went on
in a brisker tone, 'And, knowing you, your background, the kind of person you are, I suddenly realised
that, whatever problems might arise, we could work
them out together.'

Regan's head whirled crazily. Did he mean what
she thought he meant? She looked up at him. 'Just
what is it you're trying to say, Nick?' she asked in a
tight voice.

He sat down beside her, and put his hands on either
side of her face. 'I love you, Regan. I want you to
marry me. Or if it's against *your* principles to commit
yourself to a crusty bachelor like me, whatever you
want. You call the shots. I'll take what you're willing
to give. Just don't leave me.'

'I don't know, Nick,' she said slowly. 'It's hard for
me to believe that you've really changed your mind
about careers and families not mixing.'

'Do you believe I love you?'

Regan raised her eyes to his, searching the glittering grey depths for what lay behind them, trying
to read his thoughts, and her heart turned over. What
she saw there convinced her, and she knew. He *did*
mean it. He *did* love her. And he had suffered, too.
Only genuine torment could have broken down those
rigid defences of his.

'Yes,' she said at last. 'I believe you do.'

His gaze never left hers. 'Do you love me?'

She nodded. 'Yes, I love you, Nick.'

His eyes lit up. 'Then that's all that matters, isn't
it? We're two reasonably intelligent, sensible people.
We'll work it out, whatever comes.'

He reached out for her and gathered her into his arms, and she nestled against him. 'And you'll marry me?' he murmured.

She drew her head back and gazed up at him. 'Oh, yes,' she said happily. 'I'll marry you.'

He bent his head and his mouth covered hers in a slow sweet lingering kiss. As the heat gradually began to build between them, Regan became lost in the sheer joy of being in his arms. Of course they could work it out. It would be a struggle to balance family and career, but then she thought about Margaret Pierce, who'd said that all it took was an understanding husband. Nick respected her career, but he was a family man at heart who clearly wanted children. Yes, they could work it out.

Then, suddenly, he wrenched his mouth away from hers and pulled back. She blinked up at him. What now?

'Here's what we'll do,' he said in a brisk, businesslike tone. 'We'll get the licence tomorrow and get married as soon as possible. It looks as though you're all packed. You might as well move into my place right away.'

She had to smile. As usual he had it all figured out. For a moment she was tempted to argue with him, to assert her independence, but on second thoughts decided to save that for a more important occasion. Besides, his plan suited her perfectly.

'Yes, sir,' she said.

He nodded with satisfaction, then laid his hand on her cheek. 'Well, McIntyre,' he said softly. 'How do you think you'll like being Mrs Wainwright?'

She gave him an arch look. It wouldn't hurt to tease him a little. His ego could stand it. 'I'm not sure,' she said in a thoughtful tone. 'I rather like McIntyre myself.'

His eyes widened in surprise, and he set his jaw in the determined look she knew so well. Then he relaxed visibly, smoothed the hair back from her forehead and put his arms around her again.

'We can talk about that later,' he murmured in her ear. 'I've got something more important on my mind at the moment.'

His mouth covered hers again in a long tender kiss that warmed her to the depths of her being. Gradually, his hold on her tightened and the kiss became more urgent. His hand was on her breast, kneading gently, and, as he pressed himself up against her, Regan could feel the desire growing in him. She threw her arms around him, meeting his passion with everything in her.

His hands were travelling now underneath her shirt, the buttons of which had somehow come undone, and were moving over her bare breasts. He leaned down to nuzzle the valley between them, then gazed up at her.

'How about it, darling?' he said in a low voice. 'Shall we play this one by the book and wait until we're legal?'

'Don't you dare stop!' she commanded. She took his hand and put it firmly back where it was.

'Anything for you, ma'am,' he murmured, and his mouth came down on hers once again.

Life and death drama in this gripping new novel of passion and suspense

Following a vicious attack on a tough property developer and his beautiful wife, eminent surgeon David Compton fought fiercely to save both lives, little knowing just how deeply he would become involved in a complex web of deadly revenge. Ginette Irving, the cool and practical theatre sister, was an enigma to David, but could he risk an affair with the worrying threat to his career and now the sinister attempts on his life?

W●RLDWIDE

Accept 4 Free Romances and 2 Free gifts

• FROM MILLS & BOON •

An irresistible invitation from Mills & Boon Reader Service. Please accept our offer of 4 free romances, a CUDDLY TEDDY and a special MYSTERY GIFT... Then, if you choose, go on to enjoy 6 more exciting Romances every month for just £1.45 each postage and packaging free. Plus our FREE newsletter with author news, competitions and much more.

Send the coupon below at once to: Reader Service, FREEPOST, P.O. Box 236, Croydon, Surrey CR9 9EL

✄ — — — — — — NO STAMP NEEDED — — —

YES! Please rush me my 4 Free Romances and 2 FREE Gifts! Please also reserve me a Reader Service Subscription so I can look forward to receiving 6 Brand New Romances each month for just £8.70, post and packing free. If I choose not to subscribe I shall write to you within 10 days. I understand I can keep the free books and gifts whatever I decide. I can cancel or suspend my subscription at any time. I am over 18 years of age.

Name Mr/Mrs/Miss ——————————————————— EP86R

Address ————————————————————————

——————————————————————————————

—————————————————— Postcode ——————

Signature ——————————————————————————

Next month's Romances

Each month, you can choose from a world of variety in romance with Mills & Boon. These are the new titles to look out for next month.

WHEN THE DEVIL DRIVES Sara Craven
PAYMENT DUE Penny Jordan
LAND OF DRAGONS Joanna Mansell
FLIGHT OF DISCOVERY Jessica Steele
LEAVE LOVE ALONE Lindsay Armstrong
THE DEVIL'S KISS Sally Wentworth
THE IRON MASTER Rachel Ford
BREAKING THE ICE Kay Gregory
STEPS TO HEAVEN Sally Heywood
A FIERY ENCOUNTER Margaret Mayo
A SPECIAL SORT OF MAN Natalie Fox
MASTER OF MARSHLANDS Miriam Macgregor
MISTAKEN LOVE Shirley Kemp
BROKEN DREAMS Jennifer Williams
STOLEN KISSES Debbie Macomber

STARSIGN
DOUBLE DECEIVER Rebecca King

Available from Boots, Martins, John Menzies, W.H. Smith, Woolworths and other paperback stockists.

Also available from Mills and Boon Reader Service, P.O. Box 236, Thornton Road, Croydon, Surrey CR9 3RU.